"Y

Stephen whispered

"You can take it." With a final lingering kiss, Holly lay back on the blanket. For a moment she experienced the pleasure of looking at him and the desert sky at one time. "Aren't you coming down here with me?"

"Oh, I am. I was just trying to decide which night of deprivation I wanted to make up for first...."

A wave of anticipation surged through her. She hardly recognized her own husky voice when she murmured, "Let me show you what I've planned for tonight...."

And then she did. Stephen breathed her name between cries of ecstasy as the stars revolved around them.

THE AUTHOR

Although Cindy Victor has lived and traveled in many exotic places, she's happy to be back in her native California once more. Enjoying the warm climate, she's immersed in gardening and her work as a writer.

With the help of her husband, Gary, and a loquacious parrot who looks over her shoulder much of the time, Cindy has written *An Intimate Oasis,* her first romance novel. She set the story in Palm Springs, where she and Gary spent part of their honeymoon—twenty-two happy years ago. Though Cindy's had many newspaper articles and short stories published, she thinks "romances are more fun."

An Intimate Oasis

CINDY VICTOR

Harlequin Books

TORONTO • NEW YORK • LONDON
AMSTERDAM • PARIS • SYDNEY • HAMBURG
STOCKHOLM • ATHENS • TOKYO • MILAN

For my husband
and my hero:
Gary

Published May 1985

ISBN 0-373-25160-2

Printed in Canada

1

COMING TO THE END of the private swimming lesson—the fourth she'd given that Friday—Holly Hutton found herself wondering again if she'd checked all three latches of Daisy's cage before leaving the house. She'd gone home for a bite of lunch only to discover that in her absence the bird had tried to give herself a bath in her ceramic water cup, and had consequently drenched the cage floor. Holly had changed the covering and given Daisy fresh food and water, but had she locked the cage securely?

Daisy, her brother's beloved scarlet macaw, knew how to set herself free if even one of the curved metal locks was not fastened properly. If the bird was free, Holly suspected she would be wreaking havoc on the furniture in her brother's parrot-filled family room.

No one looking at the young woman who stood chest-deep in water would have guessed that she was worried. Holly seemed utterly relaxed and happy. Her light tinkling laughter and warm words of praise carried over the loud splashing of her student's activity in the pool.

Holly's pleasure reflected that of the older woman, Mary Gary, who justifiably was thrilled with her own progress. Her every kick was now vital and assertive, but like so many people of her age in this town dotted with backyard pools, Holly's student had been merely a bosom dipper. Bosom dippers climbed gingerly down into the shallow end of the pool and ventured out until they were up to their bosoms. Cooled off, they climbed out again.

But no more that passive sport for this lady. Holly knew that Mary would continue to improve her breathing and her stroke. The exercise would eventually benefit her figure and increase her sense of well-being, and ultimately, just possibly, improve her chances for a long life. Holly loved being a part of it. When she coached the elderly she felt more like a therapist than a swimming instructor.

Despite Holly's strong suspicions about what was going on at home, she wouldn't rush the lesson to its conclusion. Her student was exuberant, working hard, and deserved all the attention and encouragement Holly could give her. Anyhow, if Daisy was whittling a chair leg with her powerful beak, one minute more or less probably wouldn't make much difference.

At last Mary stopped her motions and the lesson, save for a few words of advice from Holly, was over.

"Holly, what about my breathing? I don't feel I'm doing that as well as I'm doing everything else."

"Your breathing is fine, Mrs. Gary. I can't get over you!" Holly was sincere. Her student's only problem in the water at this point was that she yearned to be a more-graceful swimmer than she was. That didn't bother Holly. Champion-class gracefulness wasn't required for Mrs. Gary to improve her health.

Then Mary Gary looked up, and shielding her eyes with her hand, spoke over Holly's head. "What do you think?" she asked gaily. "Will I swim the English channel?"

"No, but you'll do magnificent laps in this pool."

Holly turned.

A man was standing in a comfortable slouch on the pool deck. Holly knew immediately who he was. She registered that he was extremely handsome without being pretty. All straight planes and character lines. Laughter had marked him at either side of the wide mouth, while concern had lined his brow. His warm brown eyes were set deep with all sorts of crinkles fanning out and down from them, and dimples showed in his cheeks because he was smiling at her. His skin glowed with a healthy Palm Springs's tan that made his beautiful teeth appear brilliantly white. There was a deep groove in his strong masculine chin that no change in facial expression would ever alter.

Stephen Gary's straight brown hair was brushed back, but it angled to one side across his brow, and Holly suspected it would never be in the same shape ten minutes after he'd combed it. It was darkest where it lay short and close in front of his ears and where it curled slightly against the nape of his neck.

Holly thought that at least one set of pretty painted nails probably enjoyed toying with that luxuriant hair, then seductively tracing the virile jaw. And surely one fingertip would end its teasing little journey at that kissable chin cleft.

Holly recalled Mrs. Gary saying how handsome her son was. One expected a mother to claim that her son was good-looking so Holly hadn't thought anything of it. But Mary Gary hadn't been exaggerating. He was devastating.

Holly smiled back at him. She knew he was a psychologist and that his hobbies were lifting weights and climbing mountains. And hadn't his mother said that he was going deep-sea fishing in Mexico? Hadn't she said that he was leaving Sunday, the day after tomorrow?

Holly wondered if Stephen would be traveling anywhere near where her brother and sister-in-law were living in Mexico. Probably not. Still, it would be nice to tell him where Hank and Nettie were, just in case. But not right now. Right now she wanted to be ignored or "how do you do'd" quickly so she could get home.

"Did you see my breathing, Stephen?" Mrs. Gary asked.

"I saw. It was great. The best."

"Whew! Thank goodness! I've worked so hard on it. If I couldn't breathe right by now I'd need a psychologist to help me get over the disappointment, believe me."

Stephen chuckled and Holly smiled. To her relief Mrs. Gary started climbing out of the pool. She quickly followed.

Still breathing a little hard from the exertion of a job well-done, Mary reached for a towel as she introduced her son to her swimming instructor. "Holly's living in Palm Springs for a year. Wasn't I lucky to have found her?"

"Very lucky," Stephen said, putting out his hand to Holly.

Holly hadn't picked up a towel yet. "My hand's wet," she said, holding it up to show him that it was and immediately feeling foolish. He knew her hand was wet. She didn't have to give him a dripping exhibition of the fact.

Stephen didn't put his hand down. "I don't mind," he said. His deep voice sounded amused and the pleasure in his eyes suggested that she didn't have to purposely display any part of herself to him; he had noticed everything.

Holly had no choice except to shake his hand. She put her small wet hand against his large dry one and could have sworn she felt an electric shock. She drew in a much-needed deep breath, as though she had been the one working hard in the pool.

"How do you like living in the desert?" he asked. He didn't wipe his hand off when he let go of hers.

"Oh, I love it. The people here are wonderful." *And I might have to find a wonderful carpenter in the desert to repair all the damage in my brother's home if you don't let me leave in a minute.*

After two more minutes of polite conversation, she escaped and hurried toward the bathhouse. She rinsed off the chlorinated pool water hastily, then dried herself and got into her clothes in a scant minute and a half.

But despite her eagerness to get home, she paused

to take a good look at herself in the bathhouse mirror. She knew what she had seen when her eyes feasted on Stephen Gary, but what had he seen? She wasn't wearing makeup, of course. Not at the end of a full day of lessons. Her hair was wet—definitely not a plus. She didn't have nail polish on. Nail polish and many hours of being in chlorinated pools didn't go together. The bathing suit she'd been wearing was one of her prettier ones. Thank goodness for small favors. Overall, she didn't think she could have made a very remarkable impression on the man whose handshake had caused her whole body to tingle.

And yet she recalled the appreciative look in his smiling brown eyes. Since that frankly interested gaze couldn't have been brought forth because she looked good, it must have meant he simply liked the person he was being introduced to. *Well, if he likes me, that's even better than his liking my looks.* Holly picked up her things, wishing she didn't have to leave.

When she came out of the bathhouse she was wearing pale pink jeans and a matching pink knit shirt with a wide lemon-colored stripe across it. As she walked toward the patio table Stephen stood up, smiling as he looked her over appreciatively.

Mary asked Holly to sit and visit with them. Would she like an ice tea, or an end-of-the-day collins? Holly was on the verge of saying that she had to run, but when she looked again at Stephen's eyes she didn't want to move from the patio. What she saw there was a more-compelling inducement to stay than Mary Gary's words. Holly couldn't say no to that unspoken invitation; she didn't want to. "I can only stay for five minutes," she said. "Then I really must get home."

It figures, Stephen thought. He kept his face noncommittal although his mother showed her disappointment. But he could have told Mary not to get her hopes up. Holly was a mermaid. Today was Friday. Mermaids have Friday-night dates.

When his mother—always outspoken and never shy about finding an answer to what piqued her curiosity—asked Holly if she had a date to hurry to, Holly smiled and said no. It was just that she'd been out most of the day and was beginning to feel a little guilty.

Ask her to dinner tomorrow night. You don't leave for Mexico until Sunday. She can stay in all day tomorrow and won't have to feel guilty about going out tomorrow night.

Stephen thought his advice to himself was sound, but he didn't act on it. He regarded the swimming instructor and wondered why being out most of the day would cause her to feel guilty. Had she left her bed unmade? Dirty dishes in the sink? It couldn't be anything much more serious, she didn't look guilty. She looked fantastic—a California golden girl if he'd ever seen one. All honey tones, except for the color of butter streaking her wet hair. She wore it in a plain braid hanging below her strong swimmers' shoulders. Where it was pulled back from her smooth brow it was the color of lemons, not butter, and a few maverick tendrils curled softly around her small ears. One even turned up to tickle her beneath the lovely oval chin. That hair would feel good, even wet. Her hand had.

Darling ears, Stephen thought, when Holly turned her attention to Mary and presented him with her profile. He noted that he had never admired ears before. Except for a pair of unusually prominent ones his college roommate had been afflicted with and those of his black cat, Gabriel, he rarely even noticed them.

Ask her to dinner, damn it.

He didn't. He suspected it was his mother's presence that was holding him back.

"You're absolutely sure?" Mary cajoled. "Stephen and I are having dinner together, since my husband is in L.A. and I hate to eat alone. And it's sort of a going-away dinner, too. Did I tell you that Stephen is leaving for a two-week fishing trip to Mexico? That's a lot of fishing, if you ask me."

Holly smiled. Stephen was smiling, too. They both realized that Mary was talking on and on because she was still elated over how well her lesson had gone. Learning to swim was very important to her.

Stephen, not wanting Holly to be put on the spot anymore about spending the evening with them, was about to change the subject. He didn't get a chance to, though, because Mary persisted.

"Won't you join us, dear? You could go home first and attend to everything there, and then we could all go to Wally's Desert Turtle in Rancho Mirage at about eight o'clock."

Mother, you don't know when to give up, Stephen

thought. But he was a little bit in awe of Mary's perseverance. Of course she had her motives, and he knew them well. Her desire to have Holly's company at dinner tonight was inspired by the fact that her only son was thirty-four and unattached. If given the chance, Mary would choose seeing Stephen married again over waking up some morning with all her wrinkles, gray hairs and extra pounds gone. Well, at least she was discriminating. He turned his attention back to Holly. Honey, butter and lemon. Maybe a little help from the sun, but none from any bottle. Her hair had achieved perfection without chemistry and had all the hues of a plate of luscious, deftly cooked hotcakes.

As if this highly caloric image had fueled a hunger he hadn't known he had, Stephen quickly supplemented his mother's invitation to Holly. "That is a great idea, the best I've heard in a long time. And your student, Holly, is known for having great ideas. You will come with us, won't you? I'll make the reservation for whatever time is convenient for you. Eight, nine, nine-thirty?"

He stopped. More would be begging. And he did not believe in pressuring people. On the other hand, if Holly wasn't there he sensed that nothing the clever chef at Wally's could come up with would be palatable. Expertly executed cream of broccoli soup would be green-flecked chalk; filet mignon a slab of meat. He kept his look pleasantly expectant but not soulful. Best not to wear his heart on his sleeve and scare her off. *Come with us, Holly. I'll drink in the intoxicating look of you and won't require wine.*

Holly said that she would like to but really couldn't. Everyone at home would be despondent if left to amuse themselves too much in one day, was how she mysteriously put it. Kids? Stephen did not take after his mother in this regard, and would not ask. If so, they were very little kids. Holly was twenty-six and a half; he was sure of it.

He prided himself on being able to glean this sort of information from a person's face. He was seldom wrong about something as inconsequential as age or as important as character. A few gestures and words told him whether a person was an only child, a first-born, the middle sibling or youngest. Given half an hour with someone, he could tell if that person's childhood had been happy, so-so, or god-awful. Holly's had been great. She laughed like an angel. Her smile embraced the whole world. A sad childhood didn't produce that smile and laughter. Why, then, was there a certain aloofness about her. A reticence deep within her teal-blue eyes?

Stephen didn't think this restraint existed except when Holly was with men. Prey wasn't prey when with its own kind. He listened carefully as she talked to his mother. Definitely the oldest child in her family, and an achiever. Parents were aces. Something was there, though, a vulnerable quality.

Stephen looked away from her, telling himself it was a good thing he was going to Mexico. He really did need a vacation from work. He dealt with so many human problems in the course of a week he was probably conjuring them up where they didn't exist.

Holly got up to leave, and Stephen stood up, too.

Only Mary remained seated. She looked from her son to her swimming instructor and back to her son again with a quizzical expression on her face, as if she'd just thought of a fantastic idea, but one that was almost too farfetched to be imagined. Stephen grinned. His mother knew how attractive Holly was to him. When Holly left, Mary would try to get him to verbalize his attraction. Not a chance.

"It was nice meeting you, Stephen." This time Holly held out her hand to him.

Clasping her hand a second time, Stephen thought, *Let's have dinner tomorrow, without my mother. Then on Sunday we'll go to Mexico together.*

"Very nice meeting you, Holly," he said innocently.

"Have a wonderful trip," she said, smiling.

Stephen nodded. He was still holding her hand. He didn't want to go on the blasted trip, and for all he knew it was in his eyes for Holly to see. He finally let go of her hand, because holding a stranger's hand, like holding a breath underwater, could only be done for so long without causing stress. He didn't want to cause Holly stress. He wanted to kidnap her and take her out to sea on a fishing boat and to hell with fishing.

She walked away. He watched, his head cocked a little to the side as he studied her earnestly. She had a long-legged "I know where I'm going" stride. No insecurity in that walk. Good back. Good rear. Unlined, smooth-skinned heels padding over the flat white Bernardos. *Mmm, maybe I'm wrong. Maybe twenty-five and a half.*

"Isn't she a dream? Doesn't she make you think of peaches?" Mary asked, as Stephen sat down.

Stephen leaned back in his chair and clasped his hands behind his head. The profundity of his mother's question deserved careful consideration. He would not rush his answer.

"Well? Doesn't she?"

"Pancakes. With a squirt of lemon," he said matter-of-factly. Oh, that beautiful hair, that incredible blending of blond hues.

Mary Gary sighed. Stephen knew the sigh was meant to express an acceptance of her fate. She would never be a grandmother again. But he was a good son; she loved him.

2

FROM THE ENTRY HALL of her brother's home, Holly could see into the family room where the parrots were. She had a clear view of Daisy's cage. Daisy was in it. Breathing a sigh of relief, she went to greet her charges. "I'm home boys and girls! Look alive! If not for my devotion to you I'd be having dinner with Dr. Stephen Gary! The name means nothing to you but that's because you spend your lives in cages."

Holly stopped prattling. She knew she was prattling. Amazing how having keen-eyed parrots watching you with unrelenting interest caused you to talk to them as if they were people. But, Holly admitted, she hadn't told her feathered friends the truth. Devotion to their needs had nothing to do with why she wasn't having dinner with Stephen and Mary at Wally's Desert Turtle. If she was going to talk to birds, she shouldn't tell them anything less than the truth.

"I'm scared of him," she said softly to Lulu. She stood in front of the big white cockatoo's cage and waited for a response to her confession. It came as always. Lulu dipped her darling head close to the black cage bars and waited to be scratched on the back of the neck. Lulu was a love. She was terrified of all strangers, but once a person's status changed from stranger to friend it was an affair of the heart. Holly scratched the bird fondly.

"You're scared of people, too, Lu. You understand. The difference between us is that if you met Stephen you'd be awfully afraid of him at first, but eventually you'd love him. Then you wouldn't be afraid anymore. Well, with me it's just the opposite. I'm not really afraid of him now, I don't have to be. But if I loved him, even a little, that would really frighten me. Doesn't make sense, Lu? Don't ask for logic from humans."

Holly gave the bird one last scratch, then walked over to Tess and Teddy's cage. One of them had emitted a little petulant squawk as if to say, "Okay, Lulu's not the only one in the room."

Tess and Teddy were the clowns. They always hammed it up to get attention, but once they had it they refused to be touched. Now that Holly was at their cage where they wanted her to be, the two peach-faced lovebirds scrambled away to a perch at the rear of the cage. Teddy did a little song and dance, hopping about on the perch and squawking as if in glee that he'd enticed and then gotten away from the big bad human.

Holly laughed. "You two are more like me than Lulu is. You don't really want to be touched. You say, 'Look at me, like me, pay attention to me,' and then you back off."

She went on to the cage shared by a brown-throated conure and an Alexandrine ring-necked parakeet. The oddly matched pair lived in blissful cohabitation, whereas the clownish lovebirds were always squabbling. Alex, the exquisite blue-green, long-tailed parakeet, said "hello." It was so sweet, Holly said hello back in the same affectionate tone. Then she gently rubbed the side of the male bird's huge red beak, as she knew he loved her to do.

"Okay, have I forgotten anyone? Did you all eat your seeds and nuts while I was out and drink plenty of water? If you did I'll go get some crisp vegetables and fresh fruit. Would everybody like that?"

Daisy began emoting as Holly left the patio-facing family room. "I'm in love! Love is wonderful! I'm in love! Love is wonderful!"

Holly shook her head. Poor Daisy was bereft of her only love, and there was no way to explain to the heartbroken macaw that Hank would return. Daisy's sexual preference in regard to humans was so strong she wouldn't let any female, including Holly's sister-in-law, Nettie, handle her. Daisy adored Hank, and had behaved despondently for a week after he left. "I'm in love! Love is wonderful! I'm in love! Love is wonderful!"

Hearing the bird's lusty affirmation of love, Holly sighed. Daisy may not have known what she was talking about, but the words had their impact just the same. And Daisy would repeat the phrases at least twenty times before tiring of them. The effect would be to rub Holly's heart in the joyous message.

Holly didn't know why she felt so melancholy. It had been a very good day. Her students had all performed well and enjoyed themselves. As always, she felt lucky to have been so busy. She hadn't dared to imagine that when she moved to Palm Springs from Laguna Beach and took the ad out in the local paper, so many people would welcome what she had to offer.

She gave all the lessons she could handle and had reached the point where she reluctantly had to turn potential students away. There wasn't one pupil with whom she didn't enjoy spending an hour's time. They were all wonderful people to know. The lesson with Nelson Reiner, a blind boy, had made this Friday especially rewarding. Holly had felt so good at the conclusion of the lesson she'd thought that was what her work was all about. The glow of achievement all over Nelson's face was why she taught, why she wanted to go on teaching for as long as she was able.

Then there had been Mary Gary's lesson. Another success story. Mary had gone through life afraid of the water. She'd never even been on a boat because of that fear. But when her doctor advised her to take up swimming because she needed good daily exercise, all her latent courage came out and she did it. Holly applauded her.

And at Mary's she had met Stephen. Surely nothing to be sad about. Having dinner with him would not have been an unhappy experience. A conservative guess was that it would have been sublime. And she undoubtedly would have been able to carry it off like a lady, resisting the urge to gaze interminably into his eyes. She would have just pretended that she could taste the food and that he wasn't the most exciting man she'd ever met. The most handsome. The one whose voice would never be forgotten. Holly thought she could leave the desert and never come back, and for the rest of her life she would remember the thrilling stroke of Stephen's voice against her consciousness.

"Love is wonderful! I'm in love! Love is wonderrrrfullllll!"

Holly sighed and chopped up an apple. All of the babies loved apples. If she spread a little peanut butter on the pieces, a few caged parrots would think they'd died and gone to heaven.

She opened the pantry to get the peanut butter. Her brother had taped a list of bird-care chores to the pantry door. By now Holly knew the list by heart, but once in a while she glanced over the lengthy instructions to make sure she hadn't forgotten anything. One item was to always make sure that Daisy's cage was securely fastened before going out.

How Hank and Nettie loved their feathered babies. It would have prevented their spending this wonderful year in Mexico if Holly hadn't been willing to move into their home and be surrogate parent to the multispecied tribe. She finished checking the list and smiled a little as she always did when she came to the bottom of it and Hank's note. "Thanks a million, Gnat. Nettie and I love you and are more grateful than you can know."

Gnat. The horrid nickname Hank had invented to torture her with when they were young. They hadn't realized then that they loved each other and would be the best of friends for all time.

Holly took the peanut-butter-smeared apple chunks to the family room. She wondered what she would tell Hank about her feelings for Stephen Gary if she could talk to him right now. Probably nothing. Certainly not what she had told the uncomprehending cockatoo. Not that Hank would laugh at her consuming infatuation. Hank never laughed at her, or she at him, now that they were grown up. And when he called her Gnat she liked it, as one likes any warm intimacy shared repetitively with a special person.

The natural thing for her loving brother to say if she confided her feelings to him would be, "Go get him, Sis. If he's as great as you say he is, he's the right guy for my baby sister." But the way she felt today she could not "go get him."

Holly's thoughts were interrupted when Teddy threw a piece of apple out of his cage. It landed peanut-butter-side down on the floor Holly had scrubbed just the day before. She looked at the small colorful parrot and he looked right back at her as if to ask, "What are you going to do about it?" Then he turned tail and scooted to the rear perch, like any naughty boy escaping from a deserved swat on the behind.

Holly picked up the apple and put it back in the lovebirds' treat cup. She cleaned the floor, saying, "It's a good thing for you I have a forgiving nature, Teddy. I'm giving you a second chance."

But would she get a second chance with Stephen?

She sat down on a roomy round wicker chair and wondered if she would. Maybe. Her experience was that when she said no to a man's invitation he tried again, and usually again.

But this hadn't really been a man's invitation. It had been a man's mother's invitation. Perhaps he had just been politely going along with his mother's wishes.

No, Holly's intuition told her. *He wanted me to accept as much as I wanted to. He wanted to have dinner with me. His eyes said so as clearly as his words did.* There had been that lingering clasp of hands when they'd said goodbye. She looked at her hand, remembering how good it had felt in Stephen's. He had shared the good feeling. She knew he had. The clasp of hands had been a lingering one, with neither of them wanting to let go.

But he might forget about me when he's fishing in Mexico.

Yes, definitely, he would. He would if she didn't do something to keep him reminded of her. *Do it,* she urged herself. She jumped up from the wicker chair like a woman inspired and got out the phone directory.

She hurriedly flipped it open to the *G*'s. Maybe Stephen and Mary hadn't left for the restaurant yet. Perhaps it was too late for tonight but she would ask him to have dinner with her tomorrow. If they had dinner together before his vacation he'd be certain to remember her. And if by some cruel twist of fate he was busy tomorrow night, she would casually throw out something like, "Well, it was just a thought. Maybe we can get together when you get back. I'd love to hear about the fish you caught and about the one that got away."

No, she wouldn't say anything that dumb. Nor would she plan what to say. Spontaneity was always best. She would think of what to say when the time came.

Holly discovered that when hitherto unknown feelings made one search for a man's name in a phone directory, one's eyes didn't peruse the page efficiently. She knew she was having to search more than should be necessary. At least it wasn't a huge directory with tiny print. Her hands were trembling, and she was so nervous it was hard to imagine that she would actually go through with this if his number was listed and she managed to find it. If his name wasn't in the white pages, she would check the yellow pages under Psychologists or Counselors.

She didn't have to do that. At last she found his beautiful name and his memorable number. She would never forget it. Nope, she didn't even have to write it down. Maybe she should sit down. Her hands were shaking even more. This was a very gutsy thing she was about to do. She was going to go get him, at least for one dinner. One dinner would be okay. She didn't have to be afraid of that. And it was okay for her hands to shake. She would remain standing; it would allow her to pace while talking to him. Her knees were starting to quake. That was okay, too. Perfectly understandable.

It was not okay for her voice to tremble, so she cleared her throat before dialing and then tested her voice as if she was about to address a crowd through a microphone.

"Testing. One, two, three. This is Holly Hutton. I was wondering if you'd like to have dinner tomorrow night. Testing. One, two, three. Just testing. Forget I said it."

She put the phone back down on the kitchen desk, then sat down as if cowardice and self-defeat were more exhausting than courage and winning. Giving up made her want it more. There was a brass-framed picture of her brother on the desk top. Lulu was perched on his shoulder and a black cat Hank and Nettie used to own was sprawled across his lap. Somehow shy Lulu had been able to manage that proximity to a cat in order to have her picture taken.

She turned to the cockatoo and, as though expecting an answer, asked, "Why am I like this, Lulu? Why can't I have just a smidgen of courage when it comes to a man? To this man? I wouldn't care if it was any other, but do you know what being with this man would be like for me? It would be like flying when you never had before. It would be as if you were above the clouds, feeling the power of your wings and knowing you never had to come back down if you didn't want to. I know Hank would tell me to go after what I want if he was here, but I can't seem to do it. I've found Stephen's phone number, but I haven't found the fortitude."

Holly folded her arms on the desk and rested her head on them. In her mind she could see Stephen Gary so clearly, standing beside the pool looking down at her. A half smile had played on his lips, and she had known for a fleeting second that his mouth would look happy and sensuous like that before he kissed a woman. And after.

She stood up thinking. *I won't stiffen my backbone by sitting down.* She lifted the receiver, not having to look at the number again. The minutes that had gone by since she first saw it hadn't mattered. She'd memorized it with the first glance, just as she'd memorized his face, his form, his voice, his gestures.

"Be brave, Holly," she breathed fervently. Bravery wasn't alien to her. She was a scuba diver. Weak sisters didn't do that. And while karate wasn't as enjoyable a sport for her as scuba, it too required a stout heart. Actually she was a bundle of courage.

The phone in Stephen Gary's home rang once. Holly thought she might faint. It rang again. She held on to the edge of the desk for support. Her ears had picked up a strange hum. More of a drumming than a humming. *Oh, my heart.*

It kept ringing. She was sure he was home. He hadn't been dressed for going out to dinner when she saw him, so he would have had to go home to change. She didn't think she could go through with this. Maybe he was in the shower and was irritated by the incessant ringing. Maybe a girlfriend had stopped by and they were in a sensuous embrace and he was *very* irritated.

Stephen's phone clicked and there was a momentary silence. Holly's heart drummed faster.

"Hello. This is Stephen. I'm not able to come to the phone just now, but if you will leave your name and number...."

Holly had to wait for the recorder's beep before she could leave her message. She didn't want to wait or leave the message. Her insides shouted at her to hang up, and when she didn't obey they did a punishing somersault. She hated telephone-recording devices; not only were they eerie, but talking to a machine made her feel like an idiot. At least until now she'd never had to ask a machine to dinner. *Hang up! No. Be brave.*

Beep.

"Hello Stephen, this is Holly Hutton." She spoke too rapidly and too excitedly, but that was par for the course with these infernal things even if your heart wasn't beating wildly. If you didn't talk fast you wouldn't have time to leave all of your message. And the ultimate indignity was to have a stupid machine hang up on you. She hurried ahead. "You remember me, don't you? Your mother's swimming teacher?"

Oh God, how stupid could you get? They'd just met an hour or so ago and she'd had to ask that asinine question. Now, thoroughly flustered, she didn't have a prayer.

"I was wondering...I mean...I thought I'd just let you know that it was very nice meeting you! Goodbye!"

She sat back down. *Oh help. I didn't do that. This is a bad dream. Nobody could listen to that and not think I should be locked up. Why didn't I just leave my number and ask him to call me? Somebody bring me a razor blade, a noose, a can of worms.*

Holly had a vision of herself rushing to Stephen's

house and breaking in to get the recorder's cassette.

Daisy, as if maliciously gloating over her caretaker's despair, called, "I'm in love! Love is wonderrrfulllll!"

"Oh, shut up!"

Holly sat in misery for a few moments. No more sounds came from the family room. She got up and went to Daisy's cage. "I'm sorry, Daisy. Go ahead and express yourself. You do it well."

There was no earthly reason why Daisy shouldn't be exultant. She hadn't just made a horse's ass of herself.

Holly had intended to grill a chicken breast and make a fruit salad, but now she didn't want dinner. After that cool move on the phone she didn't think she deserved sustenance. But if she didn't eat she had to do something, and when she felt down she usually did one of two things: walk in the desert or swim.

She would swim. Nude. Even at the worst of times, it was greatly relaxing. And how lucky to have the total privacy in which to do it. She was not one who could ever swim nude in front of others. She had always been modest, while Hank and Nettie could go into a spa nude with five complete strangers and nonchalantly ask if anyone had read a good book lately.

But Hank and Nettie were far away. No neighbors were near enough to see over the high block wall around the yard even if she was to stand on the diving board. Even the birds on the other side of the sliding glass doors to the family room couldn't see her as she undressed, because she was in darkness and they were in light.

She mounted the board. Only the pool light lent a glow to the evening darkness. Holly knew that Hank did not approve of this. He was a born worrier and had mentioned six times that she shouldn't swim alone. "I know you're the best there is, Gnat, but it doesn't mean you can't get a cramp."

Just for five minutes, maybe ten, she promised her absent brother. She needed it desperately. And then she dove in.

Sometimes, when a dive was complete and Holly let herself glide effortlessly to the opposite end of the pool, she felt just like a mermaid.

3

STEPHEN WORKED TWO SATURDAYS a month, and he was working on this Saturday before his vacation. He hadn't thought of working weekends on his own but was glad when his clients, John and Jeannie Dunn, had brought up the possibility two years ago.

"Look, Stephen," Jeannie had stated, "we need you desperately if we're to hold this marriage together. But it's a hardship to come here on weekdays. We both have to take time off from work." John had nodded in confirmation.

Stephen hadn't needed twenty seconds to decide to be there for the Dunns on a weeknight or on Saturdays, whichever they preferred. Other couples and individuals who had not previously said that it was a struggle to see Stephen regularly because of their work were grateful to switch to Saturday hours, too. He was glad the last appointment of the day was coming to an end, but not because he was excited about the trip. He had not slept well. Dinner at the sumptuous Wally's had been excellent despite his disappointment that Holly Hutton wasn't there, but after coming home and listening to her phone message he had gone to bed thinking about her. And he couldn't stop thinking about her.

It was almost an irritation; women didn't settle themselves into his psyche this way. Had it been Holly's sensuous innocence as she moved beside his mother in the water? He hadn't seen her actually swim, but he couldn't remember the last time he'd seen a swan glide, either. You just knew that such performances complemented all creation. He had heard her laugh. He had heard her turn the homely sounds of speech into silk. Even when she spoke quickly and nervously on the telephone, her voice had been smooth and classy—pure silk. Silk, too, was the texture of her sun-warmed skin. Both wet and dry, the feel of her hand in his had been delicious.

He had lain awake thinking of why she had called and of the silk analogy. No, not silk. Silk looked terrific until you put it to good use, then it showed wear fast. Nice on the rack; didn't hold up. Holly, even with the bitter secret he'd seen tucked deep inside her wide young eyes, held up.

And so he had thought about her longer, searching for a better comparison. He decided she was clear, clean and hauntingly beautiful like the desert he loved. But like the desert she was inhospitable. She would let you trespass on the outer edges only. Go in deeper if you dared, but take along your own resources; she would be of no help.

As to the first question—why she had called—he decided she had wanted to make an appointment for counseling and had lost her nerve. That was normal. Many people had trouble taking the plunge. If she was like most she would wait awhile and call back.

What was out of the ordinary was that he had decided he wouldn't counsel her. There was no way he could see this woman objectively, counsel her dispassionately, and be of help in her life while staying out of it. She would probably call back as soon as he returned from Mexico, and when she did he would encourage her to get counseling, but not with him.

All of these thoughts had been shelved before his Saturday appointments, but he took them down and looked them over between appointments while he exercised. Stephen had to exercise. Heaven help his lean hard body if he didn't. He'd observed his bare arm while lifting a dumbbell. Had Holly's lips ever traced the flow of life through a man's skin, warming and chilling him from forearm to wrist? He doubted it.

He had not thought about Holly while first one person and then another, then a few couples, sought his help in straightening out their lives and their marriages. He never had any trouble giving himself completely to whomever he counseled. Some nights there was hardly anything left of Stephen Gary when he closed the door on his last client. Then he would walk in the desert, either near his home or out by the canyons that he loved. It was the best way to unwind. In the desert he could feel himself drink energy from the sun-leeched air. It was almost uncanny how being out-of-doors revived him. The mountains, hoarding their snow above the desert dwellers' reach, challenged his soul to rise up to their level. It never got quite that high, his soul; but the stretch was a feat.

This client, ending Saturday's sessions before Stephen's vacation, did not need him anymore. He knew it. She knew it. He also knew it would be hard for her not to come back. That was a problem with counseling: dependence. Patients experienced separation anxiety in leaving their counselor as surely as they did in leaving a warm childhood home. He felt for everyone having to go through this. But he didn't let anyone hang on to him longer than was necessary. He would not be a crutch.

"I have a feeling," the woman sitting across from him said with a calm smile, "that you're setting me back on my own feet."

Stephen returned the smile, saying, "You're already on them. And I don't think anyone can knock you off them again."

"It's hard, though. I feel like I climbed into the cupped hands of the Allstate man, and now I have to climb back out."

Stephen chuckled at the apt comparison. "But the hands didn't open up and let you drop, Carol. Climbing out is up to you. If you don't think you're ready—"

"I am!" She got up to leave, and Stephen stood to see her out. "Thank you so much, Stephen! I really do feel confident and ready for the future. May I give you a big hug? We've been through a lot together."

Stephen agreed that they had as he embraced her warmly. When this woman had first walked through his door she'd been crippled in spirit. She hadn't actually climbed into the proverbial cupped hands. Stephen had had to scoop her up. But he didn't have to worry about Carol anymore. He was worried about a young mother of two from Indio, though, who had come to him that morning with a black eye.

Carol left and Stephen listened to his recorded phone messages. Then he rewound the tape to the message he'd gone to sleep listening to the night before. The voice was like a narcotic; he wanted more and more.

"Hello Stephen, this is Holly Hutton. You remember me, don't you? Your mother's swimming teacher? I was wondering...I mean...I *thought* I'd just let you know that it was very nice meeting you! Goodbye!"

He listened to it again, then exhaled the warm moist air of a deep breath into the steeple he'd made of his fingers. *Okay, Stephen, you can listen to it ten more times or you can go for a walk in the desert.* He wouldn't be able to do that for two weeks and he'd miss it, but he'd probably hear that phone message over and over when he was out on the sea fishing.

He switched off the light, locked up and walked outside to his gracefully aging Firebird. He would go for the walk, but that didn't mean he wouldn't play the recording a few times when he got back.

It was one of Stephen's favorite months in the desert. The cold nights were past, as were the spring rains. The scorching summer months ahead would be a challenge, one he never minded. But early May was a balm—in the cool dawn he ran; he took exercise breaks throughout the day; at dusk he walked in the desert. Frequently, before bed, he swam long and hard in his pool while his cat, Gabriel, kept watch from his perch on the diving board. You could not do all of these things to keep your body lean and hard and your spirit well muscled, and not love life. But you could love life and be lonely. Good mental and spiritual health and loneliness were not mutually exclusive. Stephen knew he was lonely.

He turned the key in the ignition, looking around at the majestic landscape. He had moved there to give his clients all the privacy they could possibly want. There were social and business bigwigs among them and others who did not thrill to having it known that they required professional help with their private lives, so he had moved his office from town. But he was the one who had benefited most.

He drove toward the canyons. Funny, Palm Springs had grown up into a real town and had middle-age spread: Cathedral City, Rancho Mirage, Palm Desert. And yet you could be in the center of nowhere almost immediately no matter which direction you took. He loved that. He loved everything about Palm Springs. The San Jacinto Mountains were so exquisite. The bunny rabbits that plagued his and everyone else's lawns were so cute. The people were casual, friendly, for the most part unhurried. By and large they were happy, glad especially of where they lived. They had their assortment of troubles, which gave him his livelihood and purpose in the world, but like all else that survived in the harsh desert they were strong. Weak souls tended not to stay here permanently.

Stephen could not think of a place he'd rather live. And now, besides all else that Palm Springs offered, there was Holly. Had a sage said that when life was good it just kept getting better and better? Well, one should have.

And better still. Stephen saw the lone car parked at the side of the road. He'd seen that car yesterday in his parents' driveway. Now who could it be except hotcakes Holly, he asked himself happily. And there was the tiny speck of her golden self far out on the sweet sands of time. He picked up the binoculars he kept on the seat beside him. He always took them into the desert. You never knew what tiny beastie might entertain you in the stillness there.

Chiding himself that this was rank voyeurism and a gross intrusion on Holly's privacy—but not caring at all that it was—he honed in on her. It was like focusing on a cactus; she stood that still. She was doing nothing except experiencing the desert, letting it enrich her own existence. *We're of the same tribe, then, Holly,* he mused. He smiled toward her with his eyes and set the binoculars down. He would not be armed with them on this walk, lest she suspect that he had watched her. Just because he'd been a voyeur didn't mean she had to know it.

Later, at a calmer moment, Stephen would reflect that in all history few meetings between male and female had been less promising.

Holly had her back to him, her face to the looming wall of mountain. Knowing his desert boots couldn't have made any sound for her to hear and not wanting to startle her, he announced his presence. "Holly! Fancy meeting you out here. Do you—"

He was going to ask her if she came out there often. The words froze in midsentence. Holly had not whirled to face him as he intruded on her idyll. She had turned slowly, as if dazed, but he could see fear's shadow as a black rim framing blue-green irises. That shadow spreading from within was both a cowering thing and a creature poised to strike. Stephen supposed a doomed wild animal, prepared to struggle but knowing it could not win, would exhibit such an expression.

"Holly...."

She drew in a shuddering breath, her lips parted over dewy pearls.

"Holly. Holly, I'm terribly sorry. I shouldn't—"

"You...you bastard! No you shouldn't have! Do you know how frightening, how terrifying it is for a woman to have something like this happen?"

He did know how frightening it was, and it wasn't this frightening. His eyes narrowed with concern over her gut-wrenching fear, but he didn't vocalize his assessment. She was wounded somewhere inside. You didn't say to the wounded, *Hey, that's pretty neurotic behavior. Can't you be reasonable about what frightens you?*

He said nothing. They regarded each other. He had intended to suggest that they have dinner at Etienne's. Hardly appropriate now. A better suggestion would be that they go to his office and sit facing each other. All night. She would talk and he would listen. She would cry and he would comfort. She would put her head on his shoulder and he would stroke her hair. Rubbish. He never let his glands get mixed up with his work. He could date her or he could counsel her. He couldn't do both.

He made his choice and said, "Holly, would you forgive me and let me take you to dinner tonight?"

She was still breathing deeply, but the warning beams had switched off in the incredibly expressive eyes. She had to lick her lips before answering, and Stephen felt the intake of his own breath on seeing her tongue. He knew he'd probably seen her tongue yesterday but hadn't noticed it. That would make it the only visible part of her anatomy he hadn't committed to memory.

"I...I forgive you. And I apologize, for calling you—"

"No need," Stephen said softly. Being called "bastard"? No biggie. Psychologists took lots of abuse. But you could accept being called bastard by the whole world and still feel pain when it came from the sweet lips of Holly. Holly Hutton. It was almost too alliterative a name for a real person. Her mother must have thought she'd given birth to a pink baby doll.

"Well...I do apologize. But I won't have dinner with you."

"Why not?" he demanded. Denied the Kingdom of Heaven, a man had a right to find out what had flawed him.

"Can't. Just can't." She dipped her head down and began walking, brushing his arm as she passed as if the desert weren't wide enough to accommodate the two of them.

Okay. She had touched him first. He took her smooth bare arm in his grip, but gently, almost fearfully, not knowing if just being touched by a man would make her crack up altogether. He half expected her to lash out at him again.

But he looked down into eyes that were not fearful, only guarded. He let go, feeling ridiculous. A woman had a right to say no.

Holly placed her hand where he had held her arm. Stephen thought she would rub the arm to remove the trace of his touch. She didn't. Instead she kept her hand there, exactly as if she were keeping the feel of his hand from leaving her.

Woman, you're a strange one. Strange and hurt. He thought that if he opened his arms—just stood there near her with his arms wide—she would moor herself to the safety of him. It was something he longed to do in his office sometimes, just open himself to all the pain and replace it with comfort; give a strong shoulder to cry on. He never did. He couldn't operate that way and do his job well. But this was the desert, not his office. Why shouldn't he offer comfort if he wanted to? She wasn't his client and she wasn't going to be. "If I can't take you to dinner, Holly, could I just hold you for a minute out here? Just put my arms around you? I swear that would be all. Two ships passing in the desert but stopping to trade a little solace."

Her answer was to shove her hands in her front pockets and walk toward the road.

Stephen watched her go. He ran a hand through his thick hair in exasperation. That might just have been the most idiotic thing he'd ever done. *Cupid, when you do it, you sure stick it to us good.* Well, she could have fun with it later; tell it to a girlfriend over a cocktail. He folded his arms across his chest and watched the lady walk.

She came to a halt, looked around, then turned to come back to him.

"Why did you ask me that?"

"You hurt inside."

"Not always. I go for long stretches without feeling it. But tonight I felt it. And then you were here. It was just a bad moment. It isn't the way I usually am."

And I'm not usually six foot two. "Okay, Holly. I take it back. I don't want to put my arms around you. I'd rather take you to dinner so we can both have some good moments. How about Etienne's? Have you been there? It's very good."

Holly nodded thoughtfully. Stephen began a slow smile, taking the nod for his own sweet victory. He wasn't used to having to work this hard for a woman's company or wanting it so much.

"I understand now. You're a psychologist. And you think I telephoned you last night because I want an appointment. That's why—"

"Oh, look, Holly. I'm a psychologist, but I'm a lot of other things, too. I'm a runner. I'm a weight lifter. I'm a tennis player. I'm a history buff. I'm a guy without anyone to have dinner with on the Saturday night before he leaves for Mexico."

"Well go have dinner with your mother! Mary would love it. She adores you!"

"She's busy," Stephen said calmly. "My folks are at their best friends' anniversary party."

"Well... well go crash the party!"

Then Holly's slow laugh came. Stephen watched it well up like a blush. It said, *I know I'm being impossible, and you're being very tolerant.*

He laughed with her, unfolding his arms and putting his hands in his own pockets. Four hands in four front pockets. Stephen had the keen feeling that before long it was inevitable that her hands would slip into his, and his into hers. Back pockets.

"It's just that I don't want to get involved," Holly explained.

He cocked his head; a grin flickered merrily as he looked down at her bewitching eyes. "You don't? Well, I don't remember inviting you to."

Now she laughed out loud, tossing her head back as she did. All that expression in one sheet of straight blond hair, loose now to fan out over her shoulders. Whoever had said that hair was dead protein hadn't met Holly Hutton.

"I'll tell you what," Holly said, and he knew by the tone that he was going to be let down gently. "Not tonight. I have responsibilities at home, and I stayed away too long today."

Again. That guilt over staying out most of the day. And again he wondered what she had waiting for her at home. Little kids? No mark of a wedding band marred her finger, but you didn't know these days by the absence of that clue. She could be divorced. She could be a modern woman, fiercely independent but still maternal, adopting babies from all over the world. "When?" he asked, not at all concerned about her staying home with the babies. "Tomorrow?"

"Tomorrow?" she asked back, looking at him as if he'd just turned a bit strange.

"Right. Tomorrow."

"Uh...aren't you forgetting something? Like Mexico?"

"I'll cancel the trip," Stephen said easily. "Since it's Sunday we can spend all day together and then have dinner. If you don't want to spend too much of the day away from home we can—"

"Stephen, I scuba tomorrow," she interrupted.

Scuba. She dove. In Palm Springs? "Come and do it in my pool," he offered.

"I prefer the ocean," she said lightly and turned. Before Stephen wanted to, he found himself walking back toward the road. They walked slowly though, hands in their pockets. *If I take my hand out of my pocket will you take yours out, too, so we can hold hands?* He took his out. She didn't. He placed his gently on her back. She didn't flinch. So far so good. But did he dare to move it down, to feel the curve of her lower back and the top of that other, more-tantalizing curve? No. He raised his hand to her warm, firm shoulder instead. Just as good. Better even. A closer coziness.

"Do you dive often?" Stephen asked. It was a sport he'd never tried. If she said yes he would take it up.

"It's hard to get away, but I try to get to Laguna Beach once a week. If I leave here before dawn and get back in the evening it's okay."

He thought about it. At least two and one-half hours of tough driving each way. It was dedication to a sport, which he admired.

They were at Holly's car. "How about dinner together when you get back from your trip," Holly said, completely surprising him.

It was only a tentative step in the right direction, but Stephen was ready to leap. "How about tonight, Holly?" he asked. "I'll pick up Chinese, or a pizza and bring it to your place. You won't have to be away from home, and I won't be a guy without anyone to have dinner with."

"Okay. But it has to be an early evening, for both our sakes."

Stephen felt like crying "hallelujah" and walking on his hands. He did neither but gave her shoulder a happy squeeze. He did know how to walk on his hands quite competently, but she didn't have to witness all of his charms immediately. He would save a few to seduce her with when he got back from the trip. Oh that blasted trip. Two weeks would seem like two years. Who cared about fish anyway?

"I have to set my alarm for three-thirty," Holly said.

"I'll go home right after we eat, unless you'd like help with the dishes."

Holly grinned. "You don't have to do dishes. You do have to cook. Instead of take-out food let's grill steaks and. . . ."

The menu and division of duties were quickly planned. Holly would do the green beans, corn on the cob and sourdough garlic toast. Stephen said that in addition to grilling the steaks at her house, he would make a salad at his place and bring it over.

"That's good," Holly said. "It'll give me time to take care of all the babies."

Again, those babies. He couldn't wait to finally see them. "Should I bring a treat for the babies?" he asked, hoping for a clue. "Maybe ice cream?"

"Uh uh. They're not supposed to eat anything with sugar in it. But they'll eat some of our vegetables."

No clues in that. He decided to let the subject drop. Holly told him not to dress, because she wouldn't have time to change. He was glad. She looked terrific in her faded jeans and striped knit shirt. The ubiquitous alligator had never had it so good.

The last part of the plan was that Stephen would bring the wine and Holly would defrost a cheesecake.

Stephen chuckled, suggesting that they didn't really need all that food. Having Holly next to him over coffee would be all the sweetness he could want, but he kept that appraisal to himself.

"It'll keep us out of trouble," she said. "Remember, we don't want to get involved."

He smiled to himself, because they already were. His hand was so involved with her shoulder he hated to take a break from the coziness, but reluctantly he did. "See you in an hour, on one condition," he said.

She looked questioningly at him. What was left that they hadn't discussed?

"Give me your address."

She complied with some embarrassment.

Ahh. He knew that street and the street number. Even Gabriel knew that house, although the cat must hope—if cats can hope—that he would never see it again.

"Holly, isn't that the Mullinses' house?" He'd been to a party of theirs. Hank was a high-school art teacher; Nettie a high-school Spanish teacher. They had a passion for parrots. Big parrots. Little parrots. All different colors...babies. The parrots were definitely the coddled-and-cooed-at babies in that house. At the party Stephen had admired the somewhat out of place "child"—a lone cat. Hank had said that Gabe was getting gloomier every time a new parrot was added to the family. And Stephen, who had gone to the party with a gorgeous raven-haired doctor, had come home with both the doctor and the black cat. A good relationship had developed with the cat, whereas the doctor had been just one of those things.

"Hank's my big brother," Holly explained. "Same mother, different fathers. I'm house sitting for a year while he and Nettie are studying in Mexico. They're both on sabbatical."

"Are you twenty-six and a half?" Stephen asked almost sternly. He just couldn't believe it. He could have sworn Holly was the eldest child in her family. She looked surprised by the question, which certainly didn't have anything to do with the conversation, but she answered with one affirmative nod.

Well then, his powers of intuitive observation still

held up fifty percent of the time. "In an hour," he said, closing the car door for her. He watched her drive away.

Could you feel better about life, Dr. Gary, than you do at this exact moment? He asked himself that while walking two inches above the ground to his own car.

No.

Yes. He was going away tomorrow, and he didn't want to. And there was something else. He remembered the unspeakable terror in Holly's eyes when he'd surprised her on the desert. It had quickly dispersed; it was a secret look mirroring something Holly kept hidden from the world, and maybe even from herself. Sometimes little children had that look tucked away in their wide clear eyes if life had dealt them a severe-enough blow. So his question to himself could only be answered with a melancholy yes. He would feel better about life when Holly did. And his feet were planted firmly on the ground.

4

HOLLY HAD TAKEN ALEX out of his cage and brought him into the kitchen to keep her company while she prepared the beans and corn. He perched on a chair back, watching her with affectionate interest. She was nervous and needed company. Alex was her favorite despite the fact that he was horrendously noisy.

"Wait till you meet him," Holly told her friend. "He's even more beautiful than you and just as nice. Don't knock it. You don't find that combination in many humans. If you do they're married, or priests. I don't know why I said that. I'm not looking for a husband. I am so nervous, Alex."

She had never cooked dinner with a man before, or had a man over to dinner. Hank didn't count.

Alex screeched "kee-ak, kee-ak" in a blood-pressure-raising decibel range.

"He's got a nicer voice than you, friend." Sometimes she wondered how Nettie and Hank could stand the din. And was a parrot really happy living in a family room with two high-school teachers as companions? Nettie had said that the Alexandrine ring-necks were nuisances in their native habitats of

India and Pakistan. They destroyed crops, but not for long, because the farmers shot them. Holly took a green bean to the bird to keep him quiet. It was a trade-off, she guessed. His freedom was gone but long life and a nonviolent end were assured.

The bird ate his bean and Holly finished her chores, including setting the table. Nervousness had made her work fast. She put Alex back inside his cage and cleaned up the bits of bean he had left on the kitchen floor. She saw by the parrot-shaped clock over the stove that Stephen wouldn't be here for another half hour.

The spare time gave anxiety a boost. She was dizzied by him. He turned her emotions inside out. His hand on her back had quickened a thrill that spread throughout her body. And she'd had to go on walking to her car just as if nothing was happening inside her. Then he had put his arm around her. Nothing could have felt better than that—nothing. She would have trekked across an entire desert if she could have had his hand on her shoulder all the way. But the contact had ended quickly, proving a point she'd always suspected. The best things in life might be free but they were over in a flash. During the too-short walk to the car she had had to keep her hands in her pockets, or else she would have put an arm around Stephen's waist. And she wasn't ready to take that liberty.

She didn't know what exactly she was ready to take, or how much Stephen would offer. Maybe he was actually coming here to have dinner and nothing else. But he had the power to overwhelm her senses so that everything else would follow. Oh no, that couldn't happen. It would be her worst nightmare come to life.

Holly stopped herself. Worrying wouldn't help anything. Nothing was going to happen because she wouldn't let it. She would go for a swim.

Of course. Even five minutes would soothe her and she would shed all her tension in the pool. Five minutes. No more. Then she would put something nice on for Stephen. A simple sundress—but nice. Just because you were a human ice cube didn't mean you had to go through life wearing jeans.

She stripped quickly on the patio deck, putting jeans, shirt, panties and bra on the round glass table. No more than five minutes, she cautioned herself again. Then she'd have just enough time to shower, braid her hair, put lipstick on and get dressed. The yellow sundress.

She mounted the board eagerly and dived in. Ah yes! This was the therapy that never failed. Nobody should go through life without this heavenly relaxation. She wished—as she turned deftly and began another lap—that she could teach the whole world to swim. She didn't want anybody to miss out.

The one problem with perfect relaxation, of course, is that one loses track of time. Holly swam four laps of breaststroke, four butterfly laps, and then turned over to swim on her back.

"Holly."

She wasn't sure she had heard her name. The second time she was sure. She let all of herself below the neck sink into the water and from the neck up she was a spluttering, crimson, wide-eyed, soggy-haired, embarrassed person who wished she'd never been born.

"Holly, you can't stay in the middle of the pool forever. Come over here."

The tone of Stephen's voice told her two things: he appreciated her dismay; he wasn't going to make it easier by leaving. He wasn't smiling. He looked sympathetic. Other than that he was making no concessions.

"Come to the side of the pool," he repeated.

"No! Not until you go back inside the house!" She berated herself for not having locked the front door. Hank had told her over and over to always lock the door. And it wasn't something she needed to be told. She always did. Except tonight. When someone dizzied you and turned your emotions inside out, stupid mistakes followed.

She continued treading water, knowing that the movement of the water didn't hide anything from him. You could see a dime at the bottom of the pool from where he stood.

"The first time I saw you I thought you looked like a mermaid," Stephen said mildly, as if he could calm her by engaging her in conversation. "Now that I've seen you swim, I know you're one."

Her distress would not abate. She had not been seen naked since the onset of adulthood, except by her doctor. Doctors didn't count. She decided to reason with him. "I'm not a mermaid. I'm a person. People have feelings, including embarrassment. Please go inside the house."

"I also thought you looked like a plate of hot-cakes."

It made no sense but she was not going to question it. At last, after inanely equating her with a hot breakfast, he turned and walked away from the edge of the pool.

But he didn't go inside. With casual ease, he began to undress, striped shirt first. He placed it on the table over her shirt. One alligator playfully getting on top of another. Then the jeans, dropped over her bra and panties. Then....

She turned around. Okay. She had a game plan. When he got in she would get out. She could move faster in the water than anyone who wasn't a professional swimmer. She would run inside and lock all the doors. He could swim to his heart's content. But she was dining alone tonight, and she hoped that whatever he ate would have a little salmonella swimming in it.

Stephen mounted the diving board. Holly didn't look at him. She paddled to the side of the pool. She could hear him testing the board. "I hope it sends you right over the wall," she muttered. A new idea sprang to mind. She would grab his clothes and throw them into the pool before she ran inside the house. He deserved it.

"Holly, I don't want you to be angry about this."

She whirled and faced him, prepared to tell him what chance there was of her not being angry.

And there he was, poised on the end of the board, naked. She had forgotten about that problem. But she had forgotten, too, that the human body in its entirety and unclothed, could be beautiful. Stephen was breathtaking. Holly had seen only one other adult male in complete nudity, and his body had been ugly because his soul was ugly.

The sight of Stephen erased the memory of the other, however briefly. Holly lost her anger. She stopped being ashamed. "What are you going to do?" she asked softly.

"I'm going to dive into the pool and swim. And you'll swim with me. Then we'll get out of the pool and get dressed. I'll grill the steaks and we'll eat. Then I'll go home early, without helping with the dishes, so you can get to bed. Or, if you're still angry, I'll get down off this board and leave now, pausing only long enough to put my clothes back on."

Holly thought it through. "Dive," she said.

"BEING IN KELP is no problem, really," Holly said after a bite of cheesecake. She was able to give Stephen a rough demonstration of extricating herself from kelp while sitting in her chair. He pretended to shudder and she laughed. "So much for scuba," she said. "Now you tell me something."

He had already talked a little about family-systems therapy, and Holly had laughed at the story of Gabriel being saved from a life spent in the company of birds he was forbidden to stalk.

"Let's see," Stephen said thoughtfully. "I haven't told you yet how beautiful I think the name Holly Hutton is. I thought it was almost too pretty when I first heard it—a little artificial. But it grows on you. It's lovely."

"It grew on me, too," she said with a laugh. "It is artificial, in a way. I wasn't born with it." She told him the story. Her real name was Natalie. Everyone had called her Nat when she was little. Hank, on learning that there was such a thing as a gnat, had gleefully told everybody he could get to listen that his sister's name was Gnat. From then on the name Nat, coming out of Hank's teasing mouth, had an edge of malice to it. "I saw myself as a bug," Holly said. "It didn't make for self-confidence."

Stephen chuckled and agreed that it wouldn't. "How did you make the big leap from the insect to the plant world, so to speak?" he asked.

"Oh, we were moving to a new neighborhood, and I was determined not to go there as a gnat. I pleaded my case well and my parents said I could change my name to anything I liked."

"That was admirable," Stephen said. "And unusual. Few parents feel secure enough in their roles to let kids make important, long-range choices on their own."

"Mmm, maybe all eight-year-old kids aren't ready to make important choices, without help," Holly suggested. "My first choice for a new name was Saturn, which I thought sounded wickedly sophisticated. From then on my freedom of choice was curtailed."

"Saturn," Stephen said softly, trying the name out. "It is wicked. Would have changed your whole life."

"I know. I'd be teaching belly dancing. I'll tell you what came after that if you promise not to laugh. Or is this getting boring? When you complimented me on my name you didn't expect a whole history."

"It isn't boring. I'm enjoying the history immensely. I won't laugh," Stephen promised.

"Scarlet. My grandmother took me to see *Gone with the Wind.*"

Stephen broke his promise. Holly, affecting a simpering drawl, batted her eyes flirtatiously and asked if he wanted more coffee.

"Yes, please, Scarlet. It wouldn't have fit, but it's a whole step above Saturn."

Holly could tell that Stephen was enjoying this lengthy anecdote about her change of name, and she was enjoying confiding in him. "Well, to make a long story shortish, I would pick names and they would be rejected, or mom would pick a name and I would say no. Hank came up with Lassie. Finally, we all agreed on Holly. And do you want to know the nicest thing? The minute we made the choice they began calling me Holly and never reverted to Natalie. I really did feel important, because I'd named myself."

"Holly, that's lovely. When I met you I thought your parents must be terrific people. I guessed right."

Holly smiled. "Do you always do that? Decide what people's parents are like when you meet them?"

"It's probably an occupational hazard. And I want you to know that I think Natalie is a beautiful name, too. Your folks were just as good at name choosing as you were. Does your brother ever call you Gnat?"

"All the time."

"I'll bet you like it."

"I do."

They sat in silence a minute, just smiling and enjoying the closeness, the relaxation. Then Stephen said, "I should leave. I don't want to keep you up, and I haven't packed yet."

Holly didn't want him to go. She didn't want him to leave right now, and she didn't want him to leave for Mexico in the morning. Of course she couldn't say so.

He leaned over and kissed her cheek gently. Holly could have sworn that he knew what she'd been thinking and how she was feeling about him.

"I'll finish this cup of coffee, Holly, and in ten minutes I'm leaving."

He did.

AT THREE-THIRTY, when Stephen knew Holly's alarm would go off, he was sitting up in bed waiting to call her.

He waited till 3:31, then dialed. Holly answered on the second ring, sleepily. When she said hello, Stephen had to swallow a lump in his throat.

"Holly, this is Stephen. I didn't wake you, did I? I mean...I hope the alarm went off before the phone rang."

"It did," Holly said, still in that sleepy voice. "You didn't wake me, Stephen."

"Good. Listen, Holly, could you possibly get out of diving today?"

When she innocently asked, "Why don't you

want me to dive?" he knew that she wasn't fully awake yet. If she was wide awake she would have guessed his reason immediately.

"I'm not going to Mexico."

There was a pause before Holly asked, "Because of me?"

Stephen smiled at her forthright manner. He hated coy or evasive responses between the sexes. Holly was making him crazier about her every time she opened her mouth. "Yep," he said.

"Stephen, we'll see each other when you get back. I'll still be here. I'll be here for months."

"I'm not going to Mexico," he said again.

"Then I'm not going diving." There was not a trace of sleepiness left in Holly's tone.

Stephen fell back on the bed in jubilation as he held the phone next to his ear and wide grin. Oh, what a vacation this was going to be! Two weeks in the desert looking at a mermaid. "Holly, you just saved the lives of an untold number of fish," he said happily.

Holly laughed. "I'll set my alarm again for five-thirty so I can call my friend Linda. I think she'll be able to find someone else to dive with her."

"Great," Stephen responded, although he was too absorbed in his own happiness to be concerned about whether Linda got to go diving or not. "Since you'll be up at five-thirty, why don't I come by for you and we'll go have breakfast somewhere?"

"Okay. What time?"

"Five thirty-two?"

"Stephen...."

"Just kidding," he said, although he hadn't been. It seemed a shame to waste a couple of hours of his vacation not being with Holly, but he accepted that he couldn't have everything his way. When he thought of the winning streak he'd been on since yesterday evening he couldn't complain. He told Holly he would pick her up at nine o'clock. After she'd said goodbye and hung up he kissed the receiver.

Where will I take beautiful Holly for breakfast, he wondered. Where was the most romantic spot in the desert to have breakfast? He looked around his bedroom. It was the obvious choice, but he decided not to press his luck.

And I'd better not go too fast, he thought in stern self-admonition. He knew he had almost gone too far yesterday, and again last night. It had seemed a gift from heaven when Holly forgave him for frightening her out on the desert, and even more of a miracle when she forgave him the swimming-pool caper.

He stared at the ceiling in the darkened bedroom and saw Holly. Holly turning to face him in the desert, her wide eyes expressing much more fear than the occasion warranted. Holly in the water, nude, swimming on her back. What splendor in one woman. What perfection in a human body.

He had caught his breath and held it a long moment at the first sight of her in the pool, then exhaled slowly while fiercely cautioning himself to maintain his self-control. And even when he was naked in the pool beside her and they were swimming on their backs, by sheer force of will nothing except his arms and feet rose above the water.

He would have to be equally cautious today, he knew. Stephen warned himself to stay away from thinking about sex with Holly, and not to touch her any more than he did yesterday. He must use today and the entire two weeks to become her friend.

Stephen nodded at the conclusion of his lecture. Yep, that was the way to go with Holly. Slow. Very slow. Even slower. Don't run—crawl. And no more nude swimming; he couldn't expect the same miracle twice.

Ordinarily Holly had total control over her sleep habits. When she wanted sleep, she got it. She knew she ought to go right back to sleep after Stephen's unexpected call, because she had to be up early to phone Linda. But knowing that she should sleep and wanting to were two different things. She wanted to stay awake so she could think about Stephen and relish the sound of his voice. Only if she could take his warm, gently spoken words with her into a dream would she be willing to sleep.

Five minutes of lying awake between faded sheets that had once boasted brightly colored parrots, and she got up, took the alarm clock with her and silently padded barefoot through the house. It would be nice to linger over sweet memories and then fall asleep outside.

As Holly approached the family room, Daisy and Lulu, inside their covered cages, noisily fluffed up their wings. Holly understood. The parrots knew that someone or something was coming into their territory. They were letting the intruder know that they were aware and cautious.

"It's okay. It's only me," Holly murmured, and following her reassuring words there was silence from the large cages.

She unlocked the sliding glass door and went outside to the patio. The lower desert took a huge dip in air temperature at night at this time of year, so despite the heat of the previous day, Holly's sleeping attire of a white T-shirt and white-cotton bikini panties wasn't enough to keep her from feeling a bit cool.

She usually slept in a short nightgown or very cool summery pajamas, but once in a while she went to bed wearing the T-shirt Hank and Nettie had given her on her birthday. It couldn't be worn anywhere else, not with the ribald message it sported. Swimmers Do It for the Strokes and Kicks was custom printed in hot pink across the front of the shirt.

Hugging herself against the chill, she sat on the rough surface of the diving board and gazed down at the pool. Had the evening really happened? That they'd immensely enjoyed dining and talking together had not surprised her, but had she really swum unashamed and unafraid beside Stephen? Had she been able to look admiringly not only at his strong, graceful swimming stroke but at his lithe, tan and well-muscled body? Had she stepped nude onto this board to dive into the pool while Stephen watched her? Oh, yes. And she had smiled at his overstated but sincere compliment after she'd done an ordinary back flip. He'd said that an Olympic diving coach would weep at the opportunity being missed because she wasn't in athletic competition.

Holly smiled now, remembering how Stephen had looked as he paid the compliment. She'd discovered a new reason to be thankful for her skill in the water. She'd always seen swimming as a good means of exercising and relaxing and in recent years she'd been able to help people like Mary Gary and Nelson Reiner, which was very rewarding. But now Stephen Gary enjoyed watching her swim and dive. That was hugely rewarding.

Lying down on her stomach on the cool board and dangling a fingertip in the clear water, she marveled that she had feasted visually on the masculine perfection of Stephen's body when he, in turn, executed several effortless dives.

It all had really happened, and not once was there a moment of awkwardness or embarrassment. For a while, she swam laps while Stephen relaxed against the pool edge in the deep end. Completing one underwater lap, she had come within a foot of his maleness before veering to the side of him and reaching for the pool's edge so she could rest, too.

When she emerged beside him he said, "Now I can understand how you inspired my mother to love swimming. No one watching you swim could think that moving through water is any less natural for the human body than walking on solid ground."

There was no reference to the underwater visual intimacy that had occurred. No hint of sensuality in his manner or words. And from the moment he'd stripped to the time he was again dressed, his body didn't give physical evidence of arousal.

And yet, he was sexy just by being near her, and she could feel the magnetism between their naked bodies as they rested in the pool. She was deliciously aware that with one movement she could let go of the pool's edge, straddle Stephen's hips with her thighs, lean her head against his shoulder still glistening with water, and wrap her arms around his neck in a desire-filled embrace.

When that awareness nearly melted her insides and made her skin feel feverishly hot in the cool water, she had distracted herself from the image by saying, "When I was a child I thought it was sad that we didn't have gills. I guess I still think so. Some people would be nicer if they could spend most of their time in the water, and the world would be saner. That's silly, isn't it?"

"Not at all. It sounds very plausible. I think I'll start advising warring families who have pools to take a long daily dunk together and stay underwater for as long as possible. They won't be able to carp at each other while submerged, if you'll excuse the pun. If this becomes a tool that revolutionizes family-systems therapy, I'll give you credit for it. In print, of course."

He'd grinned, not knowing that the innocent banter had just made her realize all the more how enormously appealing he was to her. It seemed that whatever he said or did heightened that appeal and eventually her emotions were on the verge of overflowing into irrepressible desire. She hadn't wanted that to happen.

"I think most psychologists seeing this theory

coming down the pike would dismiss it as being very fishy, even if it would tip the scales toward family harmony and fewer marriages would flounder," she'd punned outrageously. "Come on, Stephen. Let's swim one more lap and then get out." She'd arced away from the edge in a dive that took her to the middle of the pool, then she glided effortlessly into the shallow end. Stephen had caught up with her and they had joined hands. Swimming with his hand holding hers, Holly had thought, *Nothing has ever felt as good as this moment. I've never felt so completely a woman. Stephen, thank you.*

Holly sat up on the diving board. She was a little chilled; dangling her finger in the water so long had even made goose bumps appear on her arms. She was going to go back inside for a robe, but looking toward the patio she decided on something better.

She and Stephen had draped their plush beach towels over chairs after drying off. She picked up the one Stephen had used, and lying down on a cushioned redwood lounge she covered herself with his towel. It didn't belong to him. It didn't smell of him. But having it over her made her feel near to him anyway. It was a very small intimacy, but it warmed her throughout. She closed her eyes and slept.

5

STEPHEN ARRIVED PROMPTLY at nine o'clock and announced that they were having breakfast in a desert canyon rather than a restaurant. Holly was delighted.

They were both wearing jeans, although Stephen's were blue and Holly's were white. By coincidence they once again had the same insignia tops on—polo players adorned their knit shirts. Stephen looked at Holly's shirt when they reached his car and said, "This is the second time in a row we've worn the same brand shirt. It's an omen. If it happens again it'll be an even bigger omen."

"What?" Holly laughed.

"It has to mean that something special is going to happen to us," he said, holding the car door open for her.

While she waited for him to walk around the car and get inside, Holly thought that he might be right. Last night he'd placed his Izod shirt over her Izod shirt and what had followed would have to be considered special in anyone's book. But what could today hold in store for them that would possibly top yesterday evening's swim and lovely dinner together? She wondered about it.

The wondering made her tremble and tingle and the feeling of excitement didn't go away the whole time they were driving to their picnic site. While Holly engaged in light conversation with Stephen, she wondered what he expected of her, what would make the day special for him. Last night he had asked nothing of her, as if intuitively aware of her fears. But she wondered if he could keep that saintly behavior up. She wondered, too, if she wanted him to behave like a saint or like a man. And how could she react this way at the thought of Stephen holding, caressing and kissing her, if she dreaded a man doing those very things?

"What do you want to eat?" Stephen asked, as they neared their destination. "Let's see if I read your mind and packed the right foods."

Holly was pretty sure that she smelled the aromas of cinnamon rolls and sausages wafting from the back of the car, and if there were sausages there were probably eggs. But she didn't want to guess wrong and disappoint Stephen, so she said, "I honestly don't know what I want." Then she thought that response applied more to their relationship than to breakfast.

"You'll know what you want when I put it in front of you?" he asked, pulling off the road.

"Right!"

"Good girl. I like that attitude."

Holly thought he couldn't possibly know that they'd just danced a little verbal jig around a double entendre. They walked into the canyon, Stephen carrying the hibachi and blanket, and Holly carrying the picnic basket. "Would you have been in Mexico already by now?" Holly asked.

"Uh uh. I would still be in the plane, thinking about you. Would you have still been in the ocean?"

"Oh no. I would have been through diving an hour ago." *And I'd be thinking about you,* she added silently. *I would have thought about you the whole two weeks you were gone.* She wanted to tell him that she was happy he'd canceled his trip, but she couldn't. She hoped he knew it without her having to say it. She would have liked to reach for his hand as they walked, but she couldn't do that either, because both of his hands were occupied with the hibachi. She certainly wanted to do something nice for him, but the only thing she could think of to do might be disappointing for him. She took the risk, saying, "I'm starved! I hope we're having orange juice, eggs, sausage, cinnamon rolls and very strong coffee!"

"We are," he said with a grin.

"I'M STUFFED!" Holly declared before taking an appreciative sip of the best coffee she'd ever tasted.

"You can't be. You eat like a bird."

"Stephen, birds eat ravenously and many times a day. I'm afraid you just gave an accurate appraisal of my main vice."

Holly put her coffee mug down on the white blanket carefully, but kept a hand on the mug, because at picnics things tended to spill. She raised her face up to the morning sun and thought happily that Stephen had chosen the nicest spot in the whole desert for their picnic. And his talent for cooking when he was in possession of nothing but eggs, a little butter, salt and pepper and a skillet was as impressive as it had been with steaks and a fully equipped kitchen.

"Do you know what?" Holly asked. "This breakfast was as special as last night's dinner. It was wonderful. I've never had a picnic breakfast before."

"Never?"

"Never, unless you count the time Hank and I snuck chocolate cake, ice cream and fudge sauce outside and had it for breakfast before our folks were up one Saturday. But even if you count that, this was better."

"I'm glad it was. You were a good sport to give up your diving and spend the day with me, Holly."

Holly looked down at her coffee mug, then back up at Stephen's beautiful brown eyes. "You gave up more," she reminded him. "I hope you won't be sorry."

"I won't be. I'm getting a whale of a lot more than the fish I gave up. Pun intended."

Holly was so enraptured, looking into his eyes, that it was a second before she even understood the joke. Then she begged, "Let's not start that fishy business again! Seriously, do you go fishing often? Is it one of your favorite sports?"

"Not often. It is a favorite. I've always wanted to catch a...."

He didn't finish the sentence, so Holly asked him what he'd always wanted to catch.

"A mermaid. But I never even saw one until Friday."

Holly smiled to let Stephen know she appreciated

the compliment, but she felt a little uncomfortable with it. *There aren't any mermaids, and I want him to see me as I really am.* The thought also occurred to her that if he was getting more than he'd given up, she didn't know what it was. Nor did she know how much she was capable of giving. The unanswered questions seemed to be hanging over her like the morning sun. She looked down.

"Are you too warm?" Stephen asked. "The temperature is rising fast."

"It is," Holly agreed. They began to put things back into the picnic basket. Rushing because she had made herself uneasy, Holly knocked over her coffee mug. There wasn't much coffee left in it, but when she tried to prevent a spill by grabbing at the falling mug, coffee poured out over her hand.

"Oh... I had to do that!" She was still nervous, but she was also relieved because there wasn't any coffee on the blanket.

"That wasn't hot, was it?" Stephen asked with concern in his voice.

"No. Just warm. And wet. Do we have another napkin?" She held her hand out so coffee dripping off it wouldn't drip onto the white blanket.

"Nope. We used them up. And they're at the bottom of the trash. Wipe your hand on my shirt."

"What...?" Holly was shocked. She began to shake her wet hand. It would be dry in a minute, and having dry coffee on her hand wouldn't be too big a catastrophe. She could handle that. She couldn't handle what he'd suggested.

"Go on. That's what I wore a dark brown shirt for.

I had you pegged as a coffee spiller when I first met you."

"You did?" Holly asked, laughing just a little.

"I sure did. I said to myself, 'Stephen, that woman is a twenty-six-and-a-half-year-old mermaid, the oldest child of terrific parents, and she spills coffee every chance she gets.'"

Holly laughed again while shaking her hand some more. She was glad he'd provided a distraction because she was still agitated by the thought of wiping her hand on his shirt. It seemed like such an intimate gesture. Her heart had suddenly started racing as if she'd just taken in a walloping dose of caffeine.

"Here, give me your hand." He took it and pulled it toward his chest, which caused Holly to lean forward a little. Stephen kept his hand over hers and rubbed it easily against his body. Not his shirt; his body. The shirt was there, of course, separating her palm and fingers from his firm flesh and warm skin. But she was breathtakingly aware of that flesh and of the crisp masculine hairs that the knit shirt prevented her from touching.

He held her hand still after rubbing it against his chest, and with that stillness she felt the beat of his heart. He had an athlete's slow pulse: it was steady, strong and sending its rhythm through her.

She broke the wordless moment with a rush of words spoken between quick breaths. "You said I eat like a bird and you're so right! Birds spill everything! Whatever goes in the beak goes on the floor, too, and sometimes on the walls. Sometimes the parrots spill their food on purpose, just for the fun of it. Yesterday—"

"Why are you so nervous?" Stephen asked, holding her hand tightly. He wore that easy reassuring look of his. It wasn't quite a smile that played on his sensuously curved lips, but it was all smile that played in his eyes.

"I'm nervous because you're holding my hand against your chest," Holly said with honest simplicity.

Stephen nodded. "It's the first time you've touched me anywhere except on my hand," he said. "When we reach out to touch someone new in our life it's natural to feel anxious. It's also natural that your touching me like this is making me sad."

"Sad?" Holly asked in surprise. It was hardly what she had expected to hear.

"Sure, it makes me very sad."

Stephen was holding her hand against his body more firmly now. The smile had left his eyes, but Holly knew that this was lighthearted, that he didn't feel at all sad, and that she was going to be teased. "Why does it make you sad?" she asked, anticipating an answer that would make her laugh.

When he replied that her touching him made him sad because she wasn't doing it voluntarily, she did laugh. And so did he. But one of his hands kept hers against his chest, while the other stroked her arm. And then he let her go. She was free to take her hand from him; free to stop feeling aroused by the most sensual body contact she had ever known.

For a moment Holly didn't move at all, but then it

was Stephen's turn to be surprised. She ran her hand leisurely over his chest. She drew slow exploratory circles with her palm around his flat muscular breasts, and then up over his clavicles. While she was exploring him in this manner her gaze was locked with his. Her own chest began to rise and fall rhythmically, as if her body was being touched. Her lips were slightly parted, while Stephen's were firmly set. He kept his hands on his thighs. Her free hand came to rest on his knee.

Stephen broke the stillness with one hoarsely whispered word, "Holly...."

"Shh...." She didn't want him to talk. She didn't want there to be any sound when she caressed his bare skin for the first time. Taking her hand from his chest, where smooth material separated it from him, she reached up to the open vee beneath his collar. With her fingers spread slightly her hand just fit there. She could feel his Adam's apple move against her fingertips, and the thrust of it moved all of her. She lifted her hand from his chest and then laid it softly against his jaw and cheek. With her thumb she outlined the marvelous cleft chin. She liked how it felt, very much, so she kept on caressing it.

"You... aren't nervous anymore," Stephen said in a low voice.

"Uh uh." Holly answered as if entranced. Her thumb kept on being chummy with his chin. She liked that chin so much. There was more that she felt like touching: his sculpted cheekbones, his beautifully shaped eyebrows, his fabulous hair. But oh, that chin. It just would not let her move on to anything else.

"Holly...."

"What, Stephen?" She smiled a little mischievously. Who was nervous now?

"You'd better stop."

"Okay."

"I'll give you an hour."

Holly laughed and took her hand from his face. But she leaned more closely to him and kissed him lightly on that glorious chin. He saw his opportunity when she did that and grabbed it, landing a return kiss on the tip of her nose.

Stephen took a huge breath, let it out, looked deep into her eyes and said, "I knew our shirts were an omen. Next time we have the same insignia near our hearts the world had better hold on tight to something!"

Holly smiled but didn't comment on that prophecy. She thought that the world might have to hold on to something whether they wore the same kind of shirts or not. She finished putting the remains of their picnic in the basket and asked, "What should we do now?" Oh Lord, that was well put. She groaned inwardly. But in a moment like this almost anything she asked would probably have come out with the sensual punch of a loaded question.

"Go horseback riding," Stephen said matter-of-factly. He added, "First we'll go back to your place so you can put sturdy shoes on and tend to the babies."

Horseback riding? Bless him. He hadn't heard any sexual suggestion in her question at all. Holly thought he was an innocent lamb, as well as being very considerate. It was so sweet of him to think about her shoes and the birds. "That's a great idea!" she enthused. "I don't ride very often, though. If you're an equestrian you'll be disappointed in me."

"I'm not and I won't be." Stephen got to his feet in one quick easy motion. He held his hand out for her to take, and when she was up and ready to leave he lifted the hibachi. "Yesterday when we walked across the sand together I had my hand on your shoulder," he began. "Remember?"

He was holding the heavy hibachi with both hands, and in his voice there was a touch of regret that he couldn't have a hand on her shoulder now. Holly said that she remembered. She was holding the picnic basket with one hand and looking down as she walked.

"I thought I could walk across a whole desert if I could just go on having my hand on your shoulder. Does my saying that bother you?"

"No, why would it?" Holly asked.

"Well, most people wouldn't want to walk across a whole desert."

Holly tossed her head back and laughed. She didn't tell him that while they had taken that first desert walk she had been thinking the same thing.

"I wanted to put my hand on your waist but I was afraid to," Stephen said.

Holly didn't answer him, but she put her arm around his waist.

They walked a few more steps.

"I wanted to put my hand in your back pocket."

"This is sort of heavy," Holly said, moving the picnic basket in front of her and taking her arm from Stephen's waist so she could hold the handle with both hands.

"Damn," he muttered. "I knew I was pressing my luck."

Holly smiled and continued to hold the basket.

"You see teens with their hands in each other's jeans pockets all the time," Stephen claimed defensively.

"Mmm, they're teenagers."

Stephen sighed. "And we're not. We're mature adults."

"Very mature," Holly agreed solemnly as they reached the car. But driving slowly back toward Hank and Nettie's house, Holly thought about how it would feel if Stephen, like a brash young teenager, was to put his hand in her jeans pocket.

Stephen, driving the car, thought it was tremendously lucky that he hadn't melted right there in the desert when she first started exploring his chest with her hand. When he'd held her hand against his chest it had felt good, but a compulsory caress wasn't the real thing. When she did it on her own, he'd sizzled just like the sausage on the hibachi. Then, when she put her hand on his bare skin, he'd all but whimpered. And what she proceeded to do to his chin had finished him off. All through it, though, he had sat erect, thankful he lived in the era of restraining clothing. His forebears, in their boxer shorts and loosely fitting slacks, must have had an awful time of it when they fell in love.

That's what's happening. I'm falling in love. Oh sure, he had fallen head over heels in lust with Holly immediately. That went without saying. But love was happening now, and it wasn't happening slowly. It was coming on like a sandstorm. Two more minutes and he'd be completely engulfed by it, he thought. *It's going to happen. The next words she says will shove me right into the middle of swirling, suffocating, maddening, inescapable, blinding love.*

"Stephen, would you like to go to a movie tonight? I've got leftovers from last night. We could have an early dinner and then catch a show, and it'll be my treat. Afterward we can go for ice cream at Häagan-Dazs."

I'm in love. Stephen smiled with infinite relief, because love didn't feel at all like a sandstorm. It felt like heaven. "Good idea," he said happily. What a day. Breakfast in the canyon, and that thing she'd done with her hand on his chest—not to mention his chin. Her arm around his waist as they walked. Horseback riding. Leftovers. Holding hands in the theater. Ice cream. And then....

"I don't know about horseback riding, though," Holly said, looking thoughtful. "It sounded great when you suggested it, but it's getting awfully warm. Isn't it too hot to take horses out? Won't they be uncomfortable?"

"Mmm, maybe. Yep, you're right." He was disappointed. Okay, it was too hot to take horses out. But Holly would have looked incredibly good in the saddle. He would have let her ride in front of him the whole time. When you fell in love with a woman it was time to see her bouncing in the saddle.

"We can do it tomorrow," Holly said. "I'm giving lessons but not until eleven. Let's go out early, before it gets hot."

Stephen wanted to whistle. He knew a fellow who owned a stable of fine horses, and he told Holly that he would arrange for two of the man's best to be available at dawn.

"Oh, good. You can call him as soon as we get to my place."

Stephen breathed deeply through slightly flared nostrils. He could just imagine the scene: the sun rising on the horizon and Holly's rear rising above the horse.

"The last time I rode was on the beach at Laguna, with my friend Linda. We went out just after dawn and it was lovely."

Stephen nodded happily. Dawn would be a little after five. Holly's first lesson was at eleven. They could ride for about five hours. Yes, and they would trot. Trotting was best for horses. It gave them a better workout than walking did, and wouldn't overtire them as a canter or gallop might. And Holly's lemon-streaked, buttery, honeyed hair would flop against her back in rhythm with the horse.

"We'll have to make it an early evening tonight, or we won't want to get up that early," Holly mused.

Stephen nodded his agreement. Ah well, you couldn't have everything. Anyhow, he had promised himself that he would proceed slowly with

Holly. An early evening was best. It was too damn hard to go slow late at night.

"We can still have the ice cream, though. What's your favorite flavor?"

"Hotcakes. Yours?"

Holly shook her head, and looked with all seriousness at Stephen. "Sometimes I think you're crazy."

"I am," he affirmed. *Crazy in love,* he added silently.

6

On their first Sunday together they spent the entire afternoon in a family room with the parrots, getting to know more about each other. The first thing Holly learned about Stephen was that this brave long-distance runner and mountain climber didn't want his fingers anywhere near a parrot's beak.

She learned, too, that he liked big-band music, jazz and anything by Cole Porter. He also favored Frank Sinatra, Barbra Streisand, Chopin and thought the Beatles had peaked with their superlative *Abbey Road* album.

Stephen learned that Holly had been to one Simon and Garfunkel and three Beach Boys concerts. She played the cello in high school but didn't keep it up afterward because she didn't think she had real talent. She loved Placido Domingo and she could listen to a good flutist for hours.

Stephen enjoyed catching fish but didn't like to cook them, though he liked to have friends over for dinner and prided himself on his chili, spaghetti sauce, pepper steak and oxtail soup. He explained to Holly that oxtail soup didn't really have oxtails in it. She thought it sounded delicious. She told him about her stuffed bell peppers. They both thought her stuffed bell peppers would be an excellent accompaniment to his pepper steak.

Holly learned that Stephen hated to wear a tie—until he actually had one on. Once he was dressed up he felt good, but every time he had to do it he would still grouse and try to get out of it.

Stephen learned that Holly had been to British Columbia, Hawaii and Acapulco, and her biggest travel yen was to see Scotland. He said he'd been to Scotland and would like to go again; it was his best trip.

She laughed and asked, "Well, what was the best thing that ever happened to you?" He said that question was too hard; it couldn't be answered. "Well, what was the worst?" she asked, and then she stopped him from answering. Her eyes had become serious and the bantering tone was gone. "Don't tell me that, Stephen. And I won't tell you anything sad about my life. Okay?"

He said, "All right. Not today. But we'll have to talk about the painful things sometime."

She quickly changed the subject, and he learned that from the second to sixth grades her best friends were identical twins. One of the twins, Linda, had stayed her best friend.

Stephen asked if she was sure her best friend was Linda. "They could have fooled you, you know."

Holly said that they had tricked her when they were young, lots of times, and it had made her feel terrible. But no matter how much the deception had hurt her she hadn't cried or pouted about it; she didn't want them to know.

"You've told me something sad," Stephen said.

"No, it wasn't," Holly protested. "It wasn't sad because it didn't destroy the friendship, and because I learned to control my emotions by not showing the twins they'd hurt me."

Stephen thought that Holly had learned to control her emotions—to hide her hurts—a little too much. But he didn't say so.

Holly said she was hungry; they hadn't eaten since breakfast. It was just five, so they had more than two hours until the movie began. They turned the leftover steak into delectable steak sandwiches and after eating drove to town. Stephen parked the car on a side street and they took a long walk. They looked in a lot of store windows, comparing their tastes in clothes, shoes, jewelry, art and furniture. Stephen had his arm around Holly's shoulders and she had hers around his waist. It was the most satisfying after-dinner walk either of them had ever had, and they both said so. They admired each other's taste in everything—even when it didn't match their own—and they said so.

Pretty soon Stephen's hand was on Holly's waist instead of her shoulder. A few times he brought it back up to gently stroke her hair or squeeze her shoulder, but mostly he kept it at her waist.

"We'd better get to the theater," Holly finally said. "If you're sure you want to see a movie," she added, looking up at him.

He didn't want to. He wanted to go back to Holly's. *Stephen, go slow.* "Sure, let's see it. It's getting great reviews."

They walked a little faster. At the theater Stephen didn't try to talk her out of paying for the tickets, and she let him buy the popcorn. They learned they both liked to sit three-quarters toward the rear of the theater, and they both hated being subjected to commercial previews when they'd paid to see a movie. They both wanted to see one of the coming attractions, which was a love story, and they didn't want to see the other, which was violent. They liked the movie, and when Holly sniffled during the sad part, Stephen squeezed her hand and leaned over to kiss her cheek. Leaving the theater feeling satisfied, they walked the long distance to the car slowly. By the time they reached it, Stephen's hand had slipped as far as it would comfortably go into Holly's back pocket, and hers was similarly tucked into his.

They admitted to each other that they couldn't eat ice cream if their lives depended on it.

Stephen drove Holly home, telling himself all the way that he was going to give Holly all the time she needed before he made love to her. He was going to be patient even if it killed him. He walked her slowly to the door and they hugged.

"I've had a wonderful day, Stephen. I'm glad you're here and not in Mexico."

"Me too."

"Stephen... do you want to come in?"

Go slow. Don't blow it. You're doing great so far. Now say good-night and leave.

"No, that's all right. It's getting late." His heartbeat accelerated just as it would have if he had been taking a lie-detector test. The polygraph would have shown that he wanted to go inside the house.

"I'll see you tomorrow morning, then." She stood on tiptoe and gave him a kiss on the mouth. It was over so quickly Stephen felt like he'd almost missed it.

"In the morning," he said a bit too cheerfully.

She watched him walk to the car and waved goodbye to him from the doorway as he drove off slowly.

They both said silently to themselves that night, in something akin to awe, *I'm in love.*

Covering the cages for the night, Holly confided to each bird that she was in love.

Stephen, scratching Gabriel behind his left ear, said, "You've got to meet her, Gabe. You'll love her."

They both went to their bedrooms feeling a little dazed. They looked in their bathroom mirrors and wondered if being in love showed on them.

They got into their beds pondering if some night soon they would get into bed together. Holly told herself probably not, because she was afraid. Stephen told himself definitely not, because Holly needed lots of time.

Holly slept. Stephen tossed and turned.

FIVE DAYS LATER, when Holly got to Linda's hilly Bohemian neighborhood above the beach, the streets seemed steeper than she remembered. She realized she had grown used to the flatlands of the lower desert now.

Linda had called and said she couldn't dive on Sunday, but she could go on Friday if Holly was free. Then they could spend the whole day and evening together. Holly had promptly cleared her calendar for Friday, rescheduling her lessons.

She was excited about seeing Linda, not just because she loved her friend and the sport. She needed to let herself go and tell somebody besides a bunch of parrots how wonderful Stephen was. And maybe, just maybe, she could also confide in Linda about her fears.

She parked her car next to Linda's little red VW. *Someday, I'll be able to come to Linda or have her come to me without remembering it. As if it had never happened.*

Holly closed her eyes and said the two brief prayers—one for herself, one for Linda. Please, God, don't let me see it in my mind again. Please, let only good things happen to Linda forever.

She opened her eyes and sighed. So far the second prayer had been consistently answered, and that was the one that mattered.

Linda opened the door looking apologetic. "Holly, I can't dive. I'm sorry kid. I feel rotten that you drove all this way. I can't even spend the whole day with you. I'm flying to San Francisco. Remember the big order I've been trying to clinch? The buyer called half an hour ago and said that if I come up and meet with her today, we'll do business. I don't like her bossy attitude, but I like what her business can do for my career. Will you forgive me, Hol?"

"Yep." Holly plopped down on a rug-covered sofa of dubious vintage. She understood and was even a little excited for her friend. Linda was a jewelry maker with a lot of talent. She needed a few good breaks and then, in the world of jewelry making, she'd be famous. This was definitely one of those breaks. And flying on the same day you dove was not safe. That was one of the first rules divers learned: the human body couldn't handle the drastic change in atmospheric pressure.

"We could make a few calls and try to find you a buddy," Linda suggested.

That idea didn't appeal to Holly. She and Linda were certified divers who had trained together. She didn't care to dive with a stranger of whose abilities and training she was uncertain. If she'd wanted to she could have gone down to the beach and found a lone diver who also needed a buddy. Laguna lifeguards were strict and tried to keep divers from going in alone, but most people who doubled up on the beach like that split up once they submerged. Holly wouldn't do that any more than she would come out of the water and get right into a plane.

"No, I don't need to dive," she said to her chagrined-looking friend. "Don't worry about it, Lin. I've got something else on my mind anyway and probably shouldn't dive. I'm as muddled as kelp."

Looking more than a little inquisitive, Linda probed, "I'm almost afraid to ask, because I think you'll say no, but is it a guy?"

A very deep breath, then an exhaled "Ye-esss."

"Holly Hutton! Miracles happen! Tell me about him quick! Is he one of your elderly students? Is he a hunk? Does he dance? Can he swim? Holly... speak!"

"Linda, you're nuts!"

"That too, but primarily I'm flabbergasted. Well...?"

"He isn't one of my students. He is a hunk. We haven't been dancing yet. He can swim. But why the dumb questions?"

"Oh, because you haven't told me that there was a male in your life since... uh, let's see, maybe the beginning of our senior year in high school. I've been waiting for this to happen as much as... as much as I suspect your mother has!"

"I suspect it has been a hard wait for mother." Holly laughed. "All right. I'll tell you about him."

"Wait! Let me get the champagne first!" Linda disappeared into the apartment's tiny kitchen to get coffee.

"His name's Stephen. He's a psychologist and has a marriage-and-family-counseling practice. But he does individual counseling and consulting for business firms, also." Linda set two steaming mugs on the tiled cocktail table, and Holly gingerly picked hers up. "Cheers," she said.

"Cheers. That's interesting. Somehow, I always pictured your winding up with a professional athlete," Linda mused. "But that's probably because I'm partial to them."

Holly smiled. Linda's boyfriend had once been a professional tennis player. Her father had been a baseball player and her younger brother had followed suit. "He's an athlete," Holly said, "but only for recreation. I'll bet you didn't picture me with a psychologist."

"No, especially since you refused to go to one when you should have."

The words were no sooner out of Linda's mouth than she looked stricken with remorse. Holly hurried to reassure her. "Don't worry about it, Lin. You're right. I should have gone to one. But let's not talk about that now."

"Right, let's not! So, you're going to pair with a psychologist! Tell me more about him."

"Linda, I'm not sure I'm going to 'pair' with anyone. That sounds like what birds do, by the way. I've had dinner with him six times and...and I guess in the past week I've been with him every waking minute that I haven't been working. Oh, Lin, it's been glorious! We've picnicked, swum, been to a movie, shopped for groceries and been to the Desert Museum together. And we went horseback riding. We've cleaned birdcages together. Did you know that cleaning birdcages can be immensely enjoyable? And another adventure into absolute bliss was washing our cars together. But the events of my week make a pretty boring recital, don't they?"

"Not when I've had to wait since our senior year for a recital like this one. I'm more excited about how you've spent the past week than I am about this evening, and this evening I'm going to enter the realm of making big bucks."

Holly smiled at her friend's enthusiasm, and also because in recounting the pleasures she'd shared with Stephen, she purposely omitted the solitary nude swim. Stephen had since stated a preference not to swim nude, which had surprised her. She still thought it was odd, but she didn't question his desire that they be demurely suited up whenever they were in the pool.

"No loving?" Linda asked nonchalantly.

Holly knew she shouldn't be startled by the brash question. Linda was Linda and would always be Linda. You could count on her to get right down to the nitty gritty of anything. Still, the question did have shock value. Holly gulped before saying, "Uh uh. No loving." She knew Linda wasn't talking about something as tame as putting your hand on a man's chest, chin or waist—or even into his back pocket.

"So, we're talking about eating, riding and swimming. And cleaning birdcages. For that you compare yourself to kelp? I'd hate to think what would happen if you two got down to serious business."

"Oh, Lin, stop! You're incorrigible! Behave yourself or you won't get another word out of me regarding Stephen."

"Okay. No more teasing. Stephen what?"

"Gary. Dr. Stephen Gary."

"Holly Gary," Linda ventured.

Holly rolled her eyes in mock despair.

"Where do you two have dinner?"

"Restaurants, and my place. One night we ate at his parents' home. They're lovely. I met Stephen when I was giving his mother a swimming lesson. Can you imagine?"

"The benefits of a good job!" Linda laughed. "It definitely makes up for your not getting sick leave and two weeks vacation. Why haven't you had dinner at his house?"

Holly wasn't surprised at the abrupt shift in the conversation. Linda was a verbal quick-change artist. In childhood both Linda's twin and Holly had had trouble keeping up with her. "I don't know why we haven't eaten at his house. It's funny, now that I think of it, that he hasn't asked me to. I know he loves to cook." Holly shrugged her shoulders a bit and gave her attention to her coffee mug for a moment.

"Maybe he's a sloppy housekeeper and doesn't want you to know," Linda suggested. "Or maybe he knows he couldn't have you to dinner in his house and not have you for the dessert. Do you think?"

"I think you think too much," Holly said, laughing. "Now tell me something about you and Kevin to give me something to think about."

"I thought you'd never ask!"

Holly watched a warm smile spread over Linda's features. Then, positively beaming, she cried, "We're getting married in September! Prepare to be a bridesmaid!"

"Linda...! Oh, Linda!" Holly fell into Linda's embrace, experiencing a joy that demanded touching because it was too big to contain in her own body. Kevin, a doctor, was a gentle knight. This was all that Holly could have hoped for.

"I wasn't going to tell you today. We're shopping for a ring next week and I was going to wait until I could flash it at you."

"I'm so happy, just so happy! For you both, Linda. I...."

She was crying. Linda knew it and clutched her in a deepened embrace. "Holly, don't. Hey, Hol... look at me, will you? So I can ask you something?"

Holly looked at the hazel eyes under a sweep of brown bangs that obscured forehead, eyebrows and half of Linda's large eyelids. She sniffed. The sudden tears had been brought on half by happiness, half by melancholy.

"Hol, maybe you really needed help in dealing with what happened to us. Would you talk to this Stephen about it? I don't mean over Scallops Provençal or when you're swimming together. Go to his office."

This Linda. Holly had to grin at practically everything she said, even when it hurt. "Don't worry about it," she said.

"But would you give it some thought?"

Holly nodded her head vigorously to set Linda's mind at peace. She would give it no thought, none at all.

"Was it my fault, Hol, that you never saw a therapist? When I asked you not to tell anyone we knew, did that keep you from getting counseling? I feel guilty about you holding the pain inside, because I got all the counseling I needed. Those weeks in therapy were a lifesaver for me."

"I knew that you wouldn't mind if I talked about it to a counselor, Lin. You encouraged me to, remember? I'm fine. Really. Don't worry." Linda didn't need to know that she couldn't possibly have gone to a counselor. How could she after promising not to tell anyone else what had happened? She had been living at home then, going to school, with no real income of her own. By all outward appearances her life was perfect, and Linda had begged her not to reveal to anyone—to her parents, Hank or any friend—that it wasn't. So if she couldn't talk to her parents about that unbearable ordeal, how could she have gone to a psychologist? When your life is supposedly unblemished you can't say, *Mom, dad, I'd like to get counseling, if you don't mind.*

"I do worry about it, Hol. We have to deal with things. We need outlets. You just bottled it up."

"There are different kinds of outlets. I took that course," Holly reminded her.

"Oh, right." Linda made a few ludicrously inept karate moves with her hands. "Okay, so you can defend yourself. You can even get hired for a bit part in a karate movie. But it seems that you can't make love. Am I right?"

"I don't know," Holly answered. "Honestly, Lin, I don't. I used to think I would never want to, that sex was hopelessly tarnished for me. Now, though, I sometimes almost want to."

"Sometimes? Almost?" Linda asked softly. "Do you mean to tell me that a man who can make cleaning birdcages a pleasure doesn't rate your saying, 'Often, I really want to'?"

"He does. I do. Often and really. But I'm scared, Linda. I'm honestly scared."

"Tell him."

Holly didn't say anything.

"Holly, will you think about it very seriously?"

Holly nodded. Linda smiled and went to warm

their coffee. The subject was closed. They could go on to Linda's wedding plans and what a lucrative pain in the rear her client in San Francisco was going to be.

Holly stayed in Laguna until Kevin picked Linda up to take her to the airport. Kevin, of course, did not know a thing about what had happened to Linda and Holly. Linda had said she would never tell him, just as she hadn't told her twin sister. "I'm not going to burden anybody who loves me with my pain," she'd said to Holly. She'd told a psychologist, and that was that.

And yet she expected Holly to be able to talk to Stephen about it. Sort of a double standard. And why did Linda think you could hold a wound closed by yourself for so long and then open it for someone to examine? You couldn't.

Nor did she want Stephen to counsel her. She knew she needed him, but not as a professional. She needed him to be her lover.

On the highway headed back toward Palm Springs, she thought of Stephen's seemingly infinite patience and understanding. His understanding of her had begun when they first met on the desert. He had known what she truly needed: to be held. Only that. That was what he had offered then and every night since. Never had he attempted to make love to her. He communicated his desire in many ways, but not in any that would make her feel rushed.

What he made her feel was cherished. It happened whenever he held her hand or put his arm around her. It happened whenever he kissed her forehead, cheek or lips. But he had never kissed her with the great passion she knew he possessed. It was as if he was holding himself back for her sake. Last night, when they kissed at her door, she'd wanted to cling to him and tell him that he didn't have to hold back. But wanting to do something and having the courage to do it were two different things.

She wanted to have that courage for him and for herself. And although she knew he would give her a lot more time, she wanted to have it now.

She looked at the wall of mountain rising up from the desert to her right. There was snow on the highest slopes. Just incredible, especially when the afternoon sun was gently baking the lower reaches. Reluctantly she kept her eyes on the road. She really wanted to gaze upon the snowy peaks, they looked so much like a mirage. That was what Stephen was like in her mind, too. His being in her life seemed like an incredible fantasy.

Mirages are illusions, a voice inside her warned. Romance is one week old. Fear of love is five years old. Ask which is stronger, the new love or the old fear. Then watch the romance—the mirage—disappear.

It won't! It isn't a mirage! It's not illusion or fantasy. Stephen and I are going to build something real. Nothing is going to disappear except my fear. I swear it!

7

IT WAS FRIDAY EVENING. Stephen had spent the day doing things he loved: tennis quite early; an hour in his weight room with his Universal Gym; and a good afternoon swim. Now, fully relaxed, he sat down on a lounge chair in the shade to read a newly published history of Rome under the Caesars. This was the kind of stuff that completely absorbed him.

He couldn't get into it. A mermaid in a wet suit kept blowing bubbles across the pages. He grinned and closed the book and let it rest against his chest. The mermaid kissed him. Mmm, sweet, sweet Holly. Holly Hutton. What a name. What a beautiful, romantic, silly name. Too silly. It was suitable for a cheerleader maybe, or a vacuous fashion model. Not for a woman who stood still in the desert at dusk, who had a rapport with elderly people and taught them to put aside their inhibitions and swim. But she could change that name. It could be changed, for instance, to Holly Gary.

Holly Gary. Not one of your great names, but not bad. His mother, who had to live with the twittery moniker Mary Gary, would do cartwheels if she even suspected he was thinking of changing Holly Hutton to a more sensible sounding Holly Gary.

He sat up and slapped the closed book against his knee, as if to jolt himself back to reality. *You just met the girl a week ago, Stephen. Are you sure you want to go serenely into old age with her?*

Nope. He wanted to find the fountain of youth and make passionate love to her for all eternity.

He thought about what he really wanted, discounting any frivolous desires caused by infatuation. He wanted to close his office door after the day's last session and find Holly in his swimming pool, her lovely limbs stretching in voluptuous strokes across the water as she waited for him. Then he would swim with her. Afterward he would cook and talk and eat with her and adore her all evening. Bedtime would be a lovefest, even when sex wasn't on the menu. Except that he would love her so much, sex would keep cropping up when it wasn't expected. Sometimes they would start the evening with sex right in the pool, then they could have a second helping in bed. And, during the hours they were apart, Holly the mermaid would go from pool to pool spreading the joy of knowing what to do with a body of water when your own body was in it. He, on dry land, would help people stay afloat in another way. And that, he decided in all seriousness, was what he wanted from his own little piece of eternity—his life.

It seemed like a reasonable goal: eternity with Holly. What he couldn't wait for was tomorrow when Holly would be with him again. But tomorrow would take longer than next Christmas to get here. And even then he would have to wait until tomorrow night, because Holly was giving lessons before lunch and all afternoon.

He wished he wasn't on vacation. If he had clients to see they would help him with the waiting. He knew he would never think about Holly while clients sat across from him singly or in pairs or in larger family units. He was always committed to each, for an hour, exclusive of all else. And his hours were hours. They weren't fifty minutes.

But why was he worrying about getting through tomorrow? What would he do with tonight? He had already played tennis, swum, worked out, and he couldn't seem to read. There were good friends that he'd been neglecting since he met Holly, but he didn't feel like talking to any of them. He felt like talking to Holly. Maybe she would come home early enough for him to see her. She could be home already. Had she said she was staying in Laguna for dinner? No, she hadn't mentioned dinner specifically. Maybe she and Linda had already had all the time they needed together. How much could two people have to say to each other? Plenty, he admitted to himself as he dialed her number. She wouldn't be home. He heard the phone ringing and imagined the birds staring at it. Was one saying hello? No, she wasn't home. He should just get into his book; it was one he'd been looking forward to reading. He listened to the phone ring some more. She could be getting out of her car right now, hearing the phone and dashing for the house.

Stephen, you've turned to mush, he chided himself, slamming the receiver down. But just because she wasn't at the house didn't mean she hadn't come back to town. She could have gone home and left again.

Stephen practically ran to his car.

She might be walking in the desert again. He did it often, so she might, too. Some people liked to unwind with a cocktail every night; others reveled in nature.

Be walking in the same place, Holly, please. He drove out of Palm Canyon somewhat apprehensively, because there were so many other places she could have chosen for a walk. He wanted so badly to see her, but he couldn't search the whole desert.

If I find you, Holly, I'm going to hold you and kiss you passionately, and I'm going to caress your breasts and the rest of you. That's all. I won't ask you to make love yet, but I'll kiss you the way I've longed to. I have to.

He got there quickly and parked, and waited. She didn't come. Alone he walked toward the canyon. He saw a lizard. The lizard didn't snub him with a quick retreat.

"Thanks, buddy. I need someone to talk to. It's about Holly. Something or somebody has hurt her so badly that she's afraid to be loved. But I know I can help her work through it and teach her that she can love completely. It's just a matter of waiting till the right time and not rushing her."

The lizard slithered off.

"Don't you want to hear the most important part?" Stephen shouted. "I've fallen in love! Listen to me, dammit! I'm really honest-to-God in love!"

Stephen stood looking at the departing lizard until

he couldn't distinguish it from its surroundings anymore. He had actually shouted the words, which for a soft-spoken man was exhilarating. Now he was willing to turn and go home and read his book. The grin of a Homo sapiens in love was spread across his face. *Well, I got that off my chest,* he thought with satisfaction. *And I didn't have to fork over sixty dollars for him to listen!*

HOLLY TENDED TO EACH of the birds's needs—rubbing one on the cheek, scratching another on the back of the neck. The brown-throated conure that shared a cage with Alex the ring-necked parakeet loved a claw massage. But Holly could only meet the birds' needs; they couldn't meet hers. She was lonely. Should she call Stephen and ask him to come over? If he hadn't had dinner she could whip up . . . ?

"Maybe he knows he couldn't have you to dinner in his house and not have you for dessert. Do you think?"

Holly walked past the phone and got her purse. She would go to his house.

He wasn't home.

She drove out Palm Canyon. Maybe he would be there. He'd said he often walked in the desert. Since they hadn't done that all week maybe he was doing it tonight. *Oh, be there! Please!*

She told herself he wouldn't be there, and yet she hoped. The day had aged and was turning gray but was even lovelier during the transformation than when it had been young. In this evening stillness and beauty, you could not quell hope.

She saw his car. Her heart raced as she began to brake. *Oh, Stephen. Stephen I'm so in love with you. I want to make love to you. I want to tonight. Help me to be able to.*

She walked out on the desert slowly and quietly, as a week ago—a lifetime ago—he had come to her. He would not be startled by her, though, and when he did see her she would run into his arms. She had the courage to show her passion now; she knew that she did.

He did not hear her. He was facing the mountains and shouting out to the unhearing canyon. Shouting that he was in love with her. Holly's heart leaped in joy and her intake of breath was so sharp it stabbed her a little. "Stephen!"

He turned. She didn't run to him. Her legs felt weak. She was going to collapse with the surfeit of emotion. Love and desire: the potent combination had never claimed her before. Who would have guessed its impact?

"I heard you, Stephen! You said. . . ." She stopped. No need to go on. Stephen knew what he had said.

"I'm glad you heard, Holly. I was telling a lizard my feelings but he took a hike. Terribly cruel thing to do when someone is expressing his deepest emotions."

"Stephen. . . Stephen I love you, too! I want to be in your arms! I. . . ."

She was. She couldn't stay still there for a second, but kissed him all over his face. She clutched at his hair, face, shoulders, arms, chest, back, buttocks. Her hands were driven by the need to claim all of him.

Her words moved around just as feverishly. She breathed them and moaned them against his mouth, his ears, his throat. "Let me love, Stephen. Stephen, help me love," she begged over and over, repeatedly interrupting herself to kiss him and taste him and explore him further with her hands. She hardly felt his doing the same to her, so frenzied and urgent was her own need to explore. The sun had left them alone out there, departing in seeming haste, as if it was mystified that they could ignore its splendor and see only each other. In the new night, Holly's innocent hand found and traced Stephen's manhood as it strained against the imprisonment of his jeans. She was surprised that stroking him there made her grow weaker. "I can't stand up," she whispered hoarsely.

He lifted her and turned toward the road. "No!" Holly cried, and she thrashed in his arms so that he hastily put her down. "Not to the car! Not to your house or mine! I want...."

She didn't know how to tell him, but she grabbed his hand and began to pull him with her farther into the desert.

"Holly, angel, not here." And Holly might as well have tried to uproot a tree as to pull him another step.

"Please! Stephen!"

"I want you just as much! More! But I am going to take you to a bed, where I can lay you down on clean smooth sheets."

He was right about the desert floor not being clean and smooth. This was not the starkly barren Mojave.

Rock, grit and scrub would sear their skin if they were to lie down. And yet she had to have it this way, so she sank to her knees in front of him.

"Holly, stand up."

She didn't answer, but the answer was no. If he could not be moved farther into the desert, she could not be taken from it. And now that she was on her knees she could touch him in a way she hadn't before; he couldn't stop her. She wrapped her arms around him and pressed her face to the force that announced his own aching need. What you love, you kiss. Holly kissed him. Softly. Lingeringly. She was on fire but knew intuitively that she must let the fire warm him slowly, not consume him in a purposeless conflagration. He groaned and clutched her head. Behind his chiseled legs, her hands moved up as far as she could reach and then stroked their way down again. Then she leaned back, her hips pressing against the heels of her sandals and her hands digging into the harsh desert floor, so she could gaze up at him. He towered over her. His look was stern. How could she have her way with him when he was all strength and conviction?

As if he were reading her mind he said, "No, Holly. I will take you to my bed. Do not lie down here."

Granite. His mind was made up. But so was hers, out of necessity. Since she hadn't been able to have her way by pleading with her hands, she would plead with words.

"I don't want to be on a bed, Stephen." She spoke very softly, but all cries and pleas carry well at night.

"Please, oh please. I don't want a bed. I don't want walls or a floor or a ceiling. I don't want electric light. A door. A pillow. Oh, please. Let me love you here. I don't think I *can* love you if you take me to your home."

"Stand up."

She leaned forward on her knees and brushed her hands off on her jeans. His tone had been as stern as his face. He was rejecting her. She would not be able to touch him again without crying, and if she cried now she would never ever stop. So she wouldn't. But she wouldn't go with him, either. No bed. No walls. No ceiling. She wouldn't because she couldn't.

She did stand up, with his help. Tears of defeat stung her eyes.

He took her hand in his, and she wanted to wrench away from him. It scalded to beg and be refused. How could they walk back to their cars holding hands after that? And how would she drive? She could barely manage walking.

He held tightly to her hand, and with his other he gently stroked her hair into place. Then, with the back of his hand he caressed the contours of her face—first one side, then the other. Her throat, too, and she thrilled where she was tender and vulnerable to the gentle pressure of his knuckles. He took his hand away from her throat and she waited hungrily for his next touch. But the caresses were over for a while. Stephen yanked his shirt out of his jeans and slowly unbuttoned it. His eyes didn't move from hers. Gently he pulled her shirt from her jeans, and when he undid the first button of her camp shirt she gasped.

"This is what you must have?" he asked softly, reaching his hand under the loosened cloth and placing it on her belly.

Night swirled around Holly and under her. She nodded. Then they walked hand in hand into the remote canyon.

They had been isolated before but now they were more so. Holly got out of her jeans, and Stephen did the same. She thought they would use their clothes for a ground cover. Awkward but adequate. Stephen did not lead her in lying down, though. He embraced her standing up and began planting urgent kisses everywhere and exploring her with his hands as she had done to him earlier. When his finger penetrated her, her legs buckled completely and he had to hold her up. Now, she thought, he would finally let her lie on the sand.

He did not. He withdrew his hand and his passionate lips simultaneously. Holly cried a soft protest. "It's all right," Stephen murmured. "It's all right, Holly darling." He supported her with one strong loving arm, and with his free hand began to slowly, rhythmically and irreversibly bring her to the threshold that waves of ecstasy would carry her over. She pierced the night with his name, over and over, and heard her own name come from him in loving echo.

He held her in silence a long while. Her head seemed to float on his chest like a leaf on water, but neither moved. She heard and felt his heart, and his breath was moist against her hair.

"That's never happened to me before," Holly said against his chest.

"I know."

"I didn't know it would feel like that. I had no idea at all what it would feel like."

"I hope you were pleasantly surprised," Stephen murmured, cradling her head against him and rocking her a little.

"Oh, I was, very pleasantly. Stephen, let's lie down now. I don't mind the roughness."

"I can't, Holly. I can't feel gentle with you from above, while the ground hurts you from below. Don't ask me."

She said no more for a minute. Then, reaching a hand between them slowly, she caressed and held him. "What about this?" she asked. "Aren't we going to let it be pleasantly surprised?"

He gasped, then trying for a light tone, said, "Oh, that. I'd forgotten all about that."

"Not me." She stroked him gently, feeling shy but comfortable with what she was doing, and her lips became a soft kiss of a smile against his chest when he groaned and pushed himself against her.

Holly tilted her face up for his hungry kiss. He possessed her with his mouth while she held his manhood against her and rubbed the yearning heat of him into her tautly arched stomach. Then Stephen's mouth released hers. His next kiss was a benediction over her ear, and she shivered as if a star made of twinkling ice had descended to tantalize the newly erotic orifice. She had not known ears were meant for anything other than hearing. Now she knew. Next he awakened her breasts, rousing each nipple to the fullness of life after a long, seemingly endless sleep.

Holly's breasts were filled with unutterable yearning, as if they hadn't received the message that the body they were part of had already been satisfied. When Stephen licked their engorged tips the cool canyon air dried them teasingly. They tingled from the quick temperature change, and Holly, not able to stand the erotic arousal anymore, uttered a soft cry and held her breasts up against Stephen's chest to rub away the electric sensations. As she did this, Stephen clasped her hard against him and voluptuously rubbed her up and down against his body. She knew that it was time for him to claim her completely, for a moment or for life, whichever Stephen decided afterward. She already knew what her decision was.

"Now, Stephen darling," Holly whispered.

"You do trust me, angel? You're not frightened? I don't...have to...if you aren't ready."

Holly's answer was to touch gently caressing fingers to the part of Stephen that she hadn't touched before. As she pressed more firmly against the soft and most-vulnerable part of him, he said her name with such hoarse urgency she thought he would collapse. Surely now he would have to lie down with her and let the starry sky glide down the sloping canyon walls until it became their cool caressing blanket.

Although she didn't anticipate its happening, Holly didn't react with surprise when Stephen's hands came down over her hips, behind her thighs, and clasping her there scooped her up. But when she was poised above him, knowing what would happen in the next instant of her life, she did gasp softly. The sound from her stopped him. He did not move her down over his manhood and claim her, and she was afraid he would change his mind and stand her back on her feet. "Now, Stephen! Let me love you now!" she cried, thrusting her hands through his thick hair and clasping his head.

And he did. He too was an athlete, and what another man could not have borne except clumsily, he did easily, slowly, gently, with exquisite rhythm. Holly was eager from the first thrust for his release into her, she craved his pleasure so much. But soon she hungered for nothing except more of the sweetly arousing friction. There was nothing to concern herself with except the blissful rise and fall of their lovemaking; it was as if she was floating effortlessly on the swell of a wave. Her second orgasm came from internal fulfillment, and as the less-explosive but more-lingering swells of it washed over her and through her she uttered his name softly, slowly, in time to the rhythm of the wavelike throbbing.

Even as Stephen's name spilled from the fullness of life within her, she felt the surge of his release. He too had crossed the sweetest of all thresholds. Then he set her down very softly and did what he'd offered to do when they had been in the desert together the first time. He held her to him. No solace was traded, for neither needed any. And Holly knew in her heart that they were not two ships merely passing in the desert. Whatever came of this, they were of and part of each other. The mirage had become a miracle—a reality.

Stephen knelt, and using his shirt he dabbed at her gently to clean her. "There, I don't want you to be uncomfortable when you're dressed." The attention made her feel both shy and grateful, but when he pressed sweet kisses to the soft flesh at the top of each thigh she felt the echo of ecstasy. He sensed it and encouraged the thrills with feather-light touches of his tongue.

When he stood back up Holly said, "I'm wanton. There doesn't seem to be any stopping me. Soon you'll be bored by my lust."

"Soon these mountains will be worn down to flat land," Stephen answered as they dressed. "Now, your place or mine, woman?"

"Yours!" Holly laughed and felt a new rush of excitement; at last she would be inside his home. It nearly made her feel giddy. She wanted to see where he sat in the morning while eating breakfast; what his dishes, place mats, coffeepot and silverware looked like. She wanted to see how he arranged his clothes in his closet and dresser drawers, and what kind and color toothbrush he preferred. Nothing too personal; she wouldn't intrude. After this Holly didn't want to go anywhere but to his home.

When she announced this preference he said, "Good. That's just where I want you. I'm going to make mad passionate salad to you, and ravish you with something sensuous and steamy and fattening."

"Oh, Stephen," she said in mock despair, "I don't know if I can take all that."

"You'll take it, woman, and you'll take it with chilled Chardonnay. Then—" he picked up one of his desert boots, putting his hand on her shoulder for support as he slipped his foot into it "—when we wake up in the morning, I'm going to have hotcakes."

Holly still didn't know what he meant by comparing her to a breakfast drowned in syrup and melted butter, but she knew she would be glad to oblige. While she leaned against him to put her shoes on she said, "Do you know what, Stephen? I thought I couldn't make love, ever. I mean...I thought I would ruin it."

"Well, you didn't," he whispered.

"I hope I'm the only woman who ever gave up her virginity in this canyon," she said proudly. "And that nobody will come after me. I really want that unique distinction."

"We could stake a claim and build a cabin. Live here and be buried on this spot," he suggested. "Eventually it would become a shrine and a tourist trap. Our descendants would conduct tours."

"Don't tease!" But she couldn't help laughing at herself, too. Granted it had been a very big deal, but there probably wasn't a spot on the globe you could stand up or lie down on where woman had not yielded to man. And that, right now, was what she felt the Earth was meant for.

They walked leisurely, holding hands. Holly thought about what he had said. Descendants. "Stephen...?"

"Hmm?"

"What if I get pregnant five seconds from now?"

That seemed to have torn it. Stephen let go of her hand and grabbed her gruffly. He continued walking with her in the circle of his arms, which meant for a few steps he was more or less dragging her along. "I hope that as of this very second you, Holly Hutton, formerly Natalie Hutton, are very thoroughly impregnated!"

"Why?" Holly laughed.

"Because then you'll have to marry me so I won't be an unmarried father. You wouldn't let me be an unmarried father, would you? That's hell on a man."

"Stephen, be serious. We just met a week ago."

"Well, Holly, a week ago I didn't hope you were pregnant."

Through her laughter Holly heard him say that she sounded like an angel. "You swim like a mermaid and laugh like an angel. I don't do anything like an angel," he said softly, pretending envy.

"Oh yes you do!" Holly assured him, and the compliment earned her a ride the rest of the distance to the road.

8

"YOU DRIVE MY CAR and I'll drive yours," Stephen said after they'd reached the road and he set her down. Holly was touched by the suggestion. He obviously needed to prolong the closeness, as did she.

"Are you sure you trust me?" she asked. "I'm still a little dazed. I might not be able to keep the wheels on the ground."

"I'll be right in front of you, so I'll function as a sobering influence," Stephen promised, as Holly handed him her keys.

"I don't have to follow you," Holly said. "I know where you live. I even went there tonight, looking for you. And since I'm making confessions, you may as well know that a few days ago I was overcome by curiosity about your home and drove past it—slowly. If I hadn't found you out here I probably would have gone back there and sat on the doorstep waiting for you into the wee hours. I felt so lovesick, like a smitten teenager."

Stephen opened the car door for her. "*I'm* smitten, so you drive carefully. If you go five miles over the speed limit I'll be tolerant, but don't let me see any tires up off the road, understand?"

Being alone in Stephen's car as the night deepened

outside the quiet town was delicious. Holly was aware that her hands were on the steering wheel that was privileged, daily, to know Stephen's touch. It was as if she could feel his hands there; even her foot on the accelerator sensed the fact that his foot belonged on it. How lovely, this closeness to him born of her imagination. She dwelled on it, smiling to herself. She was wrapping herself in the spaces Stephen inhabited, absorbing the comfort of his nearness even when he wasn't with her.

And when she looked into the rearview mirror and saw her own car with wonderful Stephen inside it, she breathed deeply with sensual awareness. *The car will levitate if I don't stop this,* she thought while her mouth parted in a euphoric smile.

Then, in a magical wink of the evening's eye, Holly was at Stephen's house.

Stephen parked beside her in the driveway and they walked toward the door holding hands. "Your car's low on gas," Stephen said. "I'd better fill it in the morning."

Nobody had ever said anything that thoughtful to her before. Was this what it was like to have a husband? She couldn't be sure, having no backlog of experience by which to measure it. She didn't answer, but squeezed his hand in grateful acknowledgment.

Maybe his seemingly infinite generosity wasn't husbandlike. There might not be any other man like Stephen, she thought. One who in a single evening would tell his feelings about you to a lizard, make love to you under the desert sky, carry you over the sand, play switch-the-cars and promise you a full gas tank.

It was almost too much to believe, and in the fullness of her appreciation, just before they got to the doorstep, Holly let go of Stephen's hand and literally jumped up on him in an embrace. He gently grabbed her under her thighs as her legs wrapped around his hips. Then he moved his hands to more comfortably clutch her taut buttocks.

"Oh, I love to touch this part of you," he said. "I love to touch every part of you. If there's any part that I haven't touched yet, would you point it out to me as soon as we're inside, so I can make up for my negligence?"

Holly hugged him and kissed his head over and over again, murmuring that he hadn't missed one part of her but she wouldn't mind if he started again from the beginning and touched all of her. As he held her in place with one hand he unlocked the door. "I seem to gravitate upward to this position," she said with a sigh against his ear.

"We don't want to overdo a good thing," Stephen chuckled. "How about if I throw you down on my bed and make love to you until you beg for mercy?"

"Uh uh. Put me down here so I can snoop around."

He pretended to sigh as he set her down in the tiled entry hall. "That's what my mother does. I hope Tildy dusted this week. She comes in Mondays and Thursdays, and I won't be held accountable for anything she neglected to get done."

Stephen turned on some lights. Holly absorbed

the aura of the home's interior slowly, savoring it as she went from one room to the next.

But before she could get very far she met Gabriel. Kneeling in the entry hall to pet the sleek black cat she murmured, "Hello, kitty. I've seen you before, in a photograph at my brother's house. Do you remember Hank and Nettie? And Lulu and Daisy and the rest?"

Gabriel slitted his eyes and inclined his pure black face against her palm. When he opened his eyes and meowed, Holly decided she was really a cat person, not a bird person. Silently she promised Gabriel that she posed no threat to him; she would not bring a parrot into his world.

Stephen was grinning, and when Holly stood up he said, "Good thing Gabe took to you or I'd be punished. When he's upset with me he waits until I'm asleep and then jumps on my chest and hisses. Then he runs off. He's not angry anymore, but I'm wide awake. Fortunately it doesn't happen too often."

"I half expected him to smell parrot on me and arch his back in hostility. I hope he won't jump on my chest in the middle of the night. I think I'd go prematurely gray."

The small awkwardness Holly felt after saying that was odd. Stephen had said, while they were still in the desert, that she was spending the night with him. Moments ago he had reiterated it by promising to fill her gas tank in the morning. So there was no mystery about the night. She was sleeping in this house. But having said so herself made her shy. She hadn't been formally asked. She became suddenly aware that there might be a certain protocol to sleeping at a man's house, one of which she was woefully ignorant. She looked down at Gabriel rubbing against her leg, instead of at Stephen. She was also aware of another lack she had, another unpreparedness: no pajamas, no toothbrush, no clean clothes.

Stephen, as if sensing her awkwardness, leaned down, turned her head to face him and kissed the tip of her nose. "Gabe won't be able to jump on your incredibly beautiful chest. You'll be in my arms."

Holly sighed at the sweetness of a nose kiss, and her nostrils flared a little. Some parts of her body were dippy little love zones, she was discovering. They knew their own measure of excitement when Stephen touched them, just as her newly discovered erogenous zones did.

Another discovery was that Stephen had the same taste in home furnishing that her brother and sister-in-law had. People in Palm Springs loved white, and their homes were likely to be painted, wallpapered, draped, carpeted, upholstered and accessorized in the wintry color. In Hank and Nettie's family room, sometimes a lone feather that wafted from a molting parrot came to rest on the white-tiled floor, and it would look to Holly as if a flower or a leaf were rising up from snow.

There were no parrots here, but Stephen was appreciative of brilliant colors, too. While the large, overstuffed upholstered pieces were starkly white, the rich brown of the hardwood floor in the living room was broken by a strikingly bold Indian rug.

The tightly-woven design was in navy, red and sky blue over a field of white. Red-and-navy throws and cushions lent the room warmth, too. Paintings attracted the eye to places high and low and in the middle of vast white walls. But best of all, in this splendid and spacious room was a life-size brass sculpture of a winged horse, rearing up and in powerful command of its body.

Holly walked over to the sculpture and touched it with an appreciative hand, awed by its metallic beauty no less than she would be if it were flesh and blood.

"It's Pegasus, isn't it? Where did you find this?"

"The artist is a friend of mine. Isn't he a genius? I'm always a bit envious of people who can create things with their hands. Do you know the story of Pegasus?"

Holly did, but vaguely. She had taken a course in Greek mythology in high school. Pegasus had sprung from the neck of Medusa when Perseus cut off the monster's head. As she admired the sculpture, Holly replied, almost dreamily, "My mythology teacher said that the moral of the story is that there's something beautiful within every creature, no matter how ugly it seems.... But I don't believe that."

"I don't, either, not stated that way. But maybe we can believe that something good will come from everything, eventually. Come on, Holly. Let's go into the kitchen."

The room was gleaming white with a plentiful assortment of copper cookware hanging decoratively from a ceiling rack. Earthenware bowls filled with various squashes and fruits testified that Stephen appreciated good fresh food. Holly was glad that a couple of dishes and a few pieces of cutlery were in the white drain rack. They satisfied her curiosity: blue-rimmed-and-dotted provincial earthenware dishes, and matching blue-plastic handles on the stainless-steel cutlery. The table in the dining nook was white and it had two blue place mats on it.

Holly touched the edge of one mat. "I keep two place mats on the table, too," she said. "Having just one place mat out makes you feel more alone, doesn't it? Stephen...?"

Holly asked him why he hadn't invited her to have dinner at his house before.

"You would never guess in a million years," he answered in the slightly amused tone of a person who is the only one in the world to know the answer to a particular question.

"You didn't think you would be able to eat dinner with me here without having me for dessert," Holly guessed.

"The truth is out," Stephen admitted. He came close to Holly and ran his strong fingers gently from her shoulders down to her hands. Then he drew each hand to his mouth and kissed it softly. "I would have wanted you for a seven-course gourmet meal," he said reflectively, pulling her hands behind his back so that her arms encircled him.

"You didn't think I was ready."

"No."

"I wasn't. Not till today. Thank you for waiting, Stephen."

"You're welcome," he murmured against her hair. "Now that you're here and ready, shall we—"

"No! I want to look around some more!"

Nothing in the house disappointed Holly. Everything captivated her. In the family room she spent a few minutes looking at old family photographs arranged on one wall. Later she would ask him who each person was. For now she was content to search the faces of Stephen's relatives for echoes of his own beautiful features.

In a small cozy den she scanned his bookshelves. "You learn a lot about people by the books they read," she explained to Stephen, talking with her head cocked sideways while she read titles. "I love mysteries and big fat biographies about politicians and their families."

Stephen reached past Holly's head to withdraw a book from the middle of a row. "If you want a good read for tomorrow night, I suggest this one," he said.

As his bare forearm came near her face she unconsciously drew in a pleasurable breath. She could just barely scent his skin, but she felt enriched sensually merely having him that close. Although she would rather have taken a small love bite of his strong, tanned and smooth-skinned arm, or tickled the tip of her nose by running it along the fine dark hair there, she took the book from him instead.

"Why not tonight?" she asked playfully to elicit the response she knew would come. Tonight was not for reading. As she fully and happily expected him to, Stephen informed her of this. He told her what tonight was for with caresses, as well as words. Holly put the book back where it belonged. "Tomorrow night won't be for reading, either," she murmured.

Stephen groaned and turned her to face him. Holding her at arm's length he said, "You have an almost-insatiable sexual appetite, which I think comes from keeping one's virginity too long. I am going to have to curb that appetite or at least sedate it temporarily."

Holly turned her head to plant a quick kiss on his wrist, then asked how he was going to do it.

"Remember that mad passionate salad? The ravishing hot meal? Get ready for what you have coming to you, woman."

Holly let her head fall back. Her lips parted as a theatrical moan escaped them. "Oooh, the Chardonnay, too?" she asked in her best Scarlet intonation. "Haven't you done enough to my body, you beast?"

Stephen looked yearningly at her without any artifice. "I'll never have done enough to your body. Not to yours, or Scarlet's, or Saturn's. There will always be more coming." He kissed her throat and chuckled lightly at Holly's genuine moan.

"Now, about that dinner," he said firmly.

"Right! Dinner!" Holly straightened and looked at him with proper seriousness. "How may I help?" she asked.

"Do you really want to be put to work or would you rather just sit and be pretty where I can see you?"

"Neither, if you don't really need me. I'd rather lie down on your bed."

"Can't wait to be there?" he asked softly, tracing a ring-size circle over the tip of one high round breast with his knuckle. The coaxed nipple hardened in recognition of the hand it worshiped, but sex was not what Holly had had in mind.

"I can't wait to see what your bedroom is like. That's the most personal room in a home. I can't wait to lie on your bed and look up at your ceiling. It's an experience I'm craving. Say it's all right with you and I'll practically fly up the stairs."

Stephen's knuckle retraced its slow circle, then went to her face to explore the soft hollow beneath the fine cheekbone. "It would hardly surprise me if you did fly," he whispered. "Of course it's all right with me. But I don't understand why you wouldn't let me take you to my bed before, Holly. Why?"

She took his hand from her face and touched her tongue to each fingertip. She blew gently on the moistened fingers, then closed them against the palm of his hand. Holding the fist she had made between her breasts she said, "Don't make me explain. I don't want to tell you. Not now."

"When?"

"Soon, perhaps. But not tonight. Tonight is heavenly. I don't want to ruin it."

He gave her a wide, indulgent smile, as if she had said something foolish. "You couldn't ruin anything to save your life. You perfect things, you don't ruin them."

She said nothing, but her eyes both thanked him

for believing that about her and begged him not to make her reveal herself now.

"Okay. Not tonight. Tonight you get to remain a mystery." He kissed her softly but deeply, and the hand that had been a gentle fist and the other opened to allow her breasts to nestle against them.

"You're wonderful." Holly sighed. "I think I'll come and help you in the kitchen. Would it be possible for you to make our dinner while holding me just the way you are right now?"

"Go lie down." Stephen laughed, giving her breasts a farewell-for-now squeeze. "I'll let you know when dinner is served."

But when Stephen came to tell Holly that they had a half hour until dinner, and to suggest they take a swim while they waited, she was not resting on his bed. She sat on a chair in front of a window that framed the barren slope of a mountain. It was a chair Stephen used for reading, comfortable and with good light during day or evening. Holly wasn't reading, although a history book, two psychology books and a newsmagazine were on the table next to her.

There were small framed photographs on it, too. Holly was holding one of the pictures; it was in a silver frame. A young woman and two little boys had smiled for the camera. While the boys obviously favored their mother, they bore traces of their father's visage in their proud and happy faces. One had not left babyhood far behind at the time the picture was taken.

Stephen put a hand on Holly's shoulder and

leaned down to look at the picture. "That's Jim on Ruth's left. The baby's name was Russ."

"How did you lose them?" Holly asked softly. She didn't really want to hear his answer. It was going to be painful—a sting reaching forward from time past. Stephen's words would sear his memory and hurt her, too. In the few seconds that elapsed before he answered, she breathed deeply and composed herself.

"They were in an automobile accident on their way to visit Ruth's parents in Redlands. It was quite a few years ago."

"Stephen... I'm sorry."

"I know you are."

They were quiet for a moment, then Stephen took the picture from her hands and set it back on the table. "Isn't it amazing what time will do? I once thought there was nothing left to live for. Now every day is precious. Today was perfect. It was even before we found each other."

Holly didn't know if it should be left at that. Perhaps she shouldn't make him talk about it. But there was a question inside her that needed asking. "How did you go on?" she asked tentatively, then continued in a rush. "I can't fathom having that much anguish in one life, Stephen. Whenever I hear something that tragic I want to cry out, to rail against the universe. I never could understand how other people have so much inner strength, how they get over their pain. I know I don't have it."

Stephen squeezed her shoulders, then took her by the hand. "Come over to the bed. Let's sit down together." He put his hand on her thigh and seemed to be studying the back of it for a moment. He took his time before saying, "I think you do have that inner strength. I sense a great deal of strength in you. You're vulnerable, and you've been hurt. But you're strong. As for all of us—how much pain we can endure and how much we can help one another get through the trauma—I've come to have great faith in people. Holly, in the majority of the species the will to survive is indomitable. Another trait I constantly find in the people I counsel is wisdom. Only most people aren't aware of how much strength or wisdom they're blessed with."

He hadn't taken his hand from her thigh, and she was looking down at him touching her. Unshed tears pricked her eyes. She turned her face to look at him, but she couldn't meet his gaze. It would have been like looking at the sun at that moment; it would have made her cry.

She didn't have to worry about meeting his eyes, because he put his arm around her and drew her to him. She pressed her face against his shoulder and he held her tighter.

"It's okay, Holly. Cry."

She did, pouring out the pain that had been hidden inside her for five long years, shielded by loneliness. That wall of loneliness had begun with a promise; her promise to Linda that she would never confide what had happened to them on that camping trip. It had fed on itself until it seemed natural; Holly had stopped imagining not being lonely. She was loved; her parents, brother, sister-in-law and friends loved her. But all of those people had their own greater and deeper loves, their sexual loves that fulfilled life.

Was she to be one of the blessed now? Stephen's arms around her and his heartbeat against her were saying that she was.

But it wasn't up to Stephen. It was up to her to put the shield aside, and she knew it. She didn't know if Stephen was right about her having courage. But she could try.

"Is it time for dinner?" she asked.

"Dinner can wait. I can keep it warm." He had gone into the room's adjoining dressing area to get a box of tissues, and Holly gratefully accepted it from him.

"Can we go into your office?"

"No. That's where I see clients. You're my lover, my friend and eventually my wife. This is where you tell me your problems."

"Stephen, I don't want to talk about it in this room. I don't want to...to defile this or any part of your home."

He took in a deep breath and shoved his hands into his pockets. She knew that he was considering it. After a shuddering sniffle she asked, "Do you believe in equality? In a couple's decision making?"

Stephen scooped up the mound of used tissues and took them to a wastebasket. "When you ask it like that I sense you're going to make the next decision for us," he said softly. He smiled at her with his eyes to let her know that she had a good chance of winning this one.

"Stephen...." Holly stopped, sighed, sniffed and used another tissue. "Stephen, let me win. I want to be strong enough to tell you about it, but not in this room. It's about a horrible thing that happened. There was a person that was so hideous...I don't want him in this room, not even in my mind."

"Let's go to my office."

"Thank you." Holly stood up. She held on to the rapidly emptying box of tissues.

"I have another box in there. You don't have to take those," Stephen said. "Tell you what. You take a few minutes to wash up—splash a little cold water on your face. I'll lower the oven temperature and open the office. Take your time. I should listen to my telephone messages. There are always plenty of those."

"Okay."

Holly watched him walk from the room. He didn't turn and look back at her. She knew he was trying to steel himself for this, as she had before she heard about his family. She ached for him because there was no way you could gird yourself against the onslaught of someone else's pain. All of a sudden she realized what a terrific drain on a person's resources being a counselor was.

She admired and respected him more than anyone she'd ever met. She wanted to live up to his early assessment of her. If he put her on a pedestal it would be a precarious position for her to maintain, but she would keep her chin up and try for balance. She believed, completely, that if she fell he would catch her.

Before going to wash up as Stephen had suggested, Holly walked over to the table by the window. She picked up the picture again and touched a finger gently to the youngest boy's innocent smile. To the woman who had loved Stephen first she said silently, *I'm finally getting over it, thanks to Stephen. And I'm going to make him happy. I promise you.*

9

Stephen turned the oven temperature down to low. The casserole would just get better while it waited. The salad was in the refrigerator with the wine.

Why do I feel as if I'm never going to have an appetite again, he wondered as he left the kitchen.

His stomach was in a tight knot. God, he didn't want to go through with this. Someone else should listen to Holly's story. It was as if she needed to have an operation, and he was to be the surgeon. It was all wrong. It even went against his concept of professionalism. But he had succumbed to her need of him and couldn't turn back now. He must listen to whatever she had to say and try to be dispassionate, professional.

Stephen had heard everything in his office. Women told him of beatings, rape, being cheated on by men they adored, of being verbally abused, of abandonment because they had reached middle age. Men told him of their hurts and fears. Children did. He listened to it all, and he could take it. Who would he be helping if he couldn't take it?

This was Holly, whom he loved heart and soul. She was going to tell him that someone—someone she had called hideous—had hurt her. And he, with his insides and emotions roiled and crazy for vengeance, would not be able to go after the bastard and do what Perseus had done to cure the evil in Medusa.

He breathed deeply as he turned the office lights on. He would play the phone messages. Such mundane activity would help calm him. He flipped the machine on. Ironically the first message had to do with Holly. His father had called to talk about an investment they shared, but had added, "Your mother and I sure enjoyed our evening with you and Holly. I don't know when I've met a lovelier or more intelligent young woman."

Or more deeply hurt, Stephen thought to himself.

The second caller, too, mentioned Holly. A friend and colleague said, "The word's going around that you're seeing the most beautiful woman in the world, Stephen. When do Sharon and I get to meet her? Call so we can all get together."

There were nine messages in all. The third, from another colleague, would ordinarily have made Stephen laugh and would have prompted an immediate return call. Bill Strand was a mature and sensitive professional who for some obscure reason liked to disguise his voice and leave outrageous messages on his close friends' telephone recorders. This time he said, "You seduced my wife, Dr. Gary. I'm going to kill you."

Stephen wasn't amused. Poor Bill had wasted his little joke on a man who wouldn't be at all amused if Richard Pryor walked into the office right now and did the best routine of his life. Nothing was funny.

Another minute and Holly would be here. The thought made the knot in his stomach grow tighter.

Stephen turned the machine off. He had listened to the voices of friends, clients, strangers and his father, but the words he had heard had slid through his mind without lodging there. These messages would all have to be listened to again.

"Stephen...?"

"Holly, I didn't hear you. Come on in and...why don't you sit over there, Holly. That's where clients sit if they come in alone."

"Where would I sit if I came in with a husband?" she asked with a nervous laugh in her voice. She tried for a game smile, too.

Stephen thought he could even see her knees tremble. He wanted to grab her and hold her and never let go—at least not until the hurt was gone from her permanently.

"You'd sit on the therapist's lap, because the husband would be me...I'd be he. I'm as nervous as you are, darling. Before you and I sit down I want to say something to you."

"Okay."

"I love you, Holly. Multiply that by a million 'love yous,' all right?"

She nodded and sat down.

Stephen sat facing her.

She looked at the plain nubby sofa to her left. "Do you ever sit with a client over there?" she asked in a small voice.

"No. Never." He said no more. He waited.

Holly drew in a big breath, let it out and talked.

She wanted to get it over with quickly. This was not a remembrance to be dwelled upon, to be told in detail slowly. In nearly a deadpan tone, in as few words as possible, she began to synthesize the horror. Holly and Linda were on a four-day trip to Big Bear Lake. They had almost left the lake early, because Linda had came down with a cold. If they had, their lives would have been much different. But they hadn't.

"It was the last night. We were packing." Holly had to stop. She put her hands over her face for a moment, then forced herself to go on.

"A man came in. We hadn't locked the cabin door. He had a gun and he grabbed my arm and pointed the gun at my head. Linda opened her mouth to say something, to reason with him maybe, and he said, 'Scream and I'll shoot your friend. Just keep quiet.' So neither of us said a word. I couldn't have anyway. I was numb. My mouth was frozen shut." She paused and looked up at Stephen. "I've always wondered... if I had screamed maybe he would have run away. If I'd only had the courage—"

"No, Holly, he probably would have used the gun. I think you instinctively knew the right thing to do. There was no lack of courage on your part." Stephen's voice was gently reassuring. "Then what happened?"

Holly took a steadying breath and folded her hands in her lap. Stephen's presence gave her the strength to continue describing the nightmarish scene. "He told me to sit down on a director's chair that faced the beds. I did. Stephen, I had to sit there while Linda . . . while he raped Linda. I just sat there and cried silently and prayed."

Holly had been looking down at her hands. She looked up to tell Stephen that she was surprised to be able to talk about it without crying, because she had cried to herself so many times. But now, when she was finally able to unburden herself to another person, she wasn't crying. But Stephen was.

She got up and went to him. Putting her arms around his neck she softly, very softly, kissed away his tears. But this unburdening was a task that she must accomplish. To do it right she had to do it thoroughly. She touched her fingertips to Stephen's cheeks to remove the last traces of his tears, then went back to her own chair.

"He got up from the bed and came over to me, pointing the gun at me again. Stephen, that was . . . that was the first time I'd seen a man naked. It made me . . . afterward . . . it made me afraid to see a man."

Stephen nodded but didn't speak. His eyes were full of compassion and understanding and pain.

"He told me to stand up and I obeyed. Then, suddenly, there were some loud noises outside. The man snapped around and grabbed his pants off the floor. I think he was cursing. There were dogs barking and he ran outside. We heard more barking and a man's shout, and then a gun went off. They killed him," Holly ended in a whisper. She shuddered and stopped talking.

"So it was over," Stephen said softly.

"Yes. It was. In a way."

"And in a way, it was just beginning for you? Because Linda had been raped and you hadn't, and because you had nobody to talk to?"

"Yes! Stephen... yes! That was so awful! Both of those things were awful!"

"You weren't responsible, Holly. You couldn't have done anything—*anything*—to prevent what happened to Linda. You didn't ask to be the one that was spared, not even when you were praying, did you?"

Holly shook her head no. She felt as if she were drinking in the words as Stephen spoke, and they cleansed a part of her that had been muddied by confusion and silence for five years. She was beginning to feel free.

"Why didn't you talk to anyone about it?" Stephen asked. "Why in heaven's name did you bottle all this up?"

"Linda... she begged me not to tell anybody. She wanted to protect herself and her family. There was no reason for them to know. We didn't even tell the whole truth to the police when they came into the cabin. Later, Linda told me she was getting counseling and that I should, too. But... I couldn't. How could I tell my family I needed counseling without telling them why I needed it? They would have worried themselves sick about me. I suppose I could have talked to a counselor on campus, without my parents knowing. I guess I was afraid to talk about it to anyone, afraid to find out just how much it had damaged me."

"Didn't you even let yourself cry about it?" Stephen asked.

"Oh yes. Often at first." When she said that she became aware once again that she wasn't crying now. Stephen had cried here in the office, but she really hadn't. It's funny," she said, her voice small but clear, "I cried in your bedroom, but that was because you lost your family and I ached for you."

Stephen cleared his throat. "Did you fear or hate men afterward, Holly?"

"No. No, I didn't. But I knew that I wouldn't let a man get close to me. I believed that I wouldn't be able to make love to a man without seeing the . . . the other one." She stopped, considering that terror she'd lived with right up to this very night. How could she have been foolish enough to fear that when Stephen made love to her she would hear that other person's voice or remember the evil look in his eyes?

"I had this irrational dread," she continued. "I thought that if we made love to each other in an ordinary room. . . . Well, I guess I had no real reason to insist we make love in the desert. I'm sorry, Stephen."

"Don't be! I'm not!"

Holly smiled tenderly at Stephen. Again she felt a rush of gratitude for having found this man with whom she could talk openly, who had a sense of humor and could joke, who cared about people and listened to them, who was unstinting with his honesty and warmth.

"I thought I'd come unglued when I told you all this," she said. "I thought I might start screaming and breaking up the furniture, like I wanted to that night. But I feel calm and at peace. You did that for me."

"I was afraid I'd do the same thing," Stephen admitted. "How is Linda now?"

Holly made a thumbs-up sign with both hands. "She's wonderful! She's going to be married in September! I just found out today. Kevin is one of the best people I've ever known. I love him."

Now Stephen smiled. "You love people—people in general—easily, don't you?"

Holly nodded. She was silent a moment before musing, "Isn't it strange that I told you the whole story without breaking down? It isn't hard for me to cry, as you saw earlier."

"No, it isn't strange," Stephen assured her.

"Well, then, isn't it strange that I feel so good sitting across from you? When I came in here I wanted to be with you on the sofa, to be able to cling to you. But now I feel as if we're touching right this second. We're touching intimately, really we are, even though I'm over here and you're over there. Isn't that strange?"

Again Stephen shook his head and said no.

"Welll...." Holly began, and then she clasped her hands over her stomach. "Isn't it strange that I'm ravenously hungry? Can you believe I still have a truck-driver's appetite, after all we've been through? Please say yes so I can bolt from this room and head straight for your kitchen."

Stephen chuckled and said he believed it, but with mock sternness, added, "You can't leave yet."

"I can't?"

"No. You can't leave the counselor's office without paying the fee."

"And what does the counselor charge?" Holly asked. She was sitting on the edge of her chair as if waiting for Stephen to say ready, set, go.

"For you, three words."

"I'll give you four." Holly's voice was barely above a whisper, and when Stephen raised his eyebrows questioningly, she paid up.

"I love you, Stephen."

"I've been up for about nineteen hours," Holly said, after swallowing a bite of the most delectable casserole she'd ever tasted. It had green beans, onions, chicken, bean sprouts, water chestnuts and cream of mushroom soup in layers, over which was a topping of cheddar cheese and French fried onion rings. When Stephen had served this steaming fare Holly had nearly devoured it with her eyes. Now that her hunger was partially sated she could speak contemplatively. "You'd think I'd crave sleep, not food." She took another bite.

"You can go right to bed after we've finished. I'll do the dishes and tidy up."

"Sounds good to me," Holly confessed. "But please don't rush me. I'm nowhere near ready to hang up my fork."

Stephen shook his head as if in dismay and said, "To think I fell in love with her for her slender figure."

Finally, Holly admitted that she was stuffed. Stephen pulled her chair out, and wrapping his arms around her when she stood up, kissed her head, nape and shoulder. "Feel free to use my toothbrush." With a love pat on her rear he dismissed her from the table.

Before going to the bedroom, Holly went into the living room. Only front-lawn spotlights illuminated the spacious room. She walked up to the winged steed. Its expression was aristocratic, and Hellenistic vision seemed to be hidden behind the unseeing eyes. Holly stroked the metallic yet somehow living creature. Yes, something good did come of everything, eventually, just as Stephen had said.

His toothbrush was blue, the kind with shorter bristles in the middle than in the outer rows. Holly used it, then nearly dove into the delicious bed. Insomniacs the world over might have envied the rapidity with which slumber kissed her good-night.

But she awakened shortly thereafter. Stephen was in bed with her, his arms encircling her. "Mmm, what time is it, darling?"

"You just turned into a pumpkin," he answered softly.

"That time? Then I have hours left to sleep." That was nice, like an unexpected gift that turned out to be just what she'd been desiring.

"Unless you want to go eat some more," he teased, patting her naked stomach. His hand moved downward "Or do something else."

Holly yawned.

"I thought you'd turn me down," Stephen murmured.

"I'll make it up to you. I'll cook you the best

breakfast and serve it to you here, or by the pool. In the bathtub. On top of Pegasus. Wherever you like." She made this offer in a sleepy voice, in phrases interspersed with yawns.

"Just so it's hotcakes," he seemed to purr against her hair. "Now go back to sleep."

Holly closed her eyes, intending to follow his good advice. She thought dreamily of making him the best hotcakes in the world when morning came, then squeezing orange juice for him. Bacon and eggs, too, if he had bacon. Eggs. She thought of eggs. Eggs in shells. Eggs come from birds. Parrot eggs. Amazon, cockatoo, lovebird, ring-neck parakeet and conure eggs.

Holly sat up. "Stephen."

"Nmmmh?"

"Are you asleep?"

"Mmm."

"I have to go home! I forgot to do something!"

"Tomorrow. Do it tomorrow."

"No, I have to do it right now! I have to cover the birdcages! Hank said at least six times that the most important thing is to cover the cages at night."

Stephen reached a hand up to her bare shoulder and tried to lure her into lying back down. "Holly, my darling, in a half-dozen hours it won't be night anymore. You'll cover them tomorrow night."

"No, really, I have to. Nettie said so, too, and it's the one thing underscored in red on my bird-chore list. Nettie said that when caged birds are used to being covered at night it's bad for them not to be. The covers protect them from drafts; they're very susceptible to colds and pneumonia. And if they aren't covered they feel nervous. They feel exposed to danger in the night. It can cause neurosis."

Stephen groaned and brought his hand down from Holly's shoulder to cover his face. "Neurosis? Neurosis?" He groaned again, louder, and turned over, then covered his head with the pillow. "Tell them to meditate for twenty minutes and call me in the morning," he muttered from beneath the pillow.

Holly got out of bed. "Don't be upset with me, please," she said. "I have to go. I get neurotic, too, if I don't fulfill a responsibility. And these are Hank and Nettie's babies. You wouldn't believe how—"

"I believe, I believe." He started to get out of bed.

"Oh Stephen, stay here. I'll go by myself. Really, it's okay."

"Nope. You're my responsibility."

"But—"

"We'll go in my car," he said.

They got into their clothes quickly but didn't bother with shoes. When Stephen opened the front door, Gabriel slipped out before them. Holly went out next thinking how lovely it was to be outdoors barefoot after midnight.

Stephen locked the door as the cat, sensing that a midnight ride was in order, stood poised in anticipation by the car door.

"The joke's on you buddy," Stephen said as Gabriel jumped onto the car seat.

10

Holly floated into the Bath and Bed Boutique on Thursday afternoon with a wallet full of hard-earned cash and a love-inspired, what-the-heck nonchalance about spending it. She knew just what she wanted: satin sheets.

Her blissful state must have shown on her face because the platinum-blond saleswoman, while checking the price of a set of king-size, pearl-gray satin sheets and pillowcases, said, "I'll bet he's terrific!"

Holly was surprised, but as she reddened slightly she laughed and asked, "Does it show that much?"

"Honey, when you walked in here I thought it must be Valentine's Day, but my wall calendar tells me February is long gone." The woman was using bifocals that hung from her neck by a gold chain, and peering at Holly through them she added, "You do look like a young lady making her first purchase of sensuous sheets."

"I am! It is my first. And yes, it is Valentine's Day. It's been moved to May," Holly said impulsively.

"And are these for your place or his? Or am I being too inquisitive?" The woman was slipping the tissue-wrapped sheets into a huge plastic bag.

You're being much too inquisitive, Holly thought, but her nonchalance about spending the money on satin sheets was accompanied by a glowing willingness to talk about her love. Actually, she would not have minded going on national television at that moment to tell anyone who would listen that Stephen was going to spend the weekend with her. With her and a lot of parrots. And he was bringing his cat.

"Mine!" she enthused. "And if I look like it's Valentine's Day today, I'll probably look like it's Christmas tomorrow."

"Or Columbus Day," the woman said, sighing. "You've discovered a brand-new world. How I envy you. Well, I was young and in love once." A wistful look of romantic nostalgia sparkled in her heavily made-up eyes.

"Aren't you in love anymore?"

The woman looked surprised by Holly's frank question. Considering the confidences they had already shared, though, Holly didn't think her question was out of line. And she really wanted to know the answer. The older couples she admired had kept their loves strong. She could say with certainty that her parents were still in love, and that Stephen's parents were.

"Why, yes, come to think of it. I am," the woman said reflectively. "But after forty years together... well, he'd call me an old fool if I put satin sheets on the bed."

Too bad, Holly thought, but she just said thank you

and goodbye and walked out of the store. *In forty years I'll put satin sheets on our bed, and Stephen will call me his mermaid, his angel and his hotcake.*

She floated to her car, slid into it and flew home.

Tomorrow was coming. Beautiful, heavenly tomorrow. Stephen would come over right after work and would stay with her for the entire weekend. A week ago they hadn't known quite how to work that out. Holly had wanted so much to spend a weekend together, and because she had to take care of the parrots the logical thing was for Stephen to stay with her. But he had said he would feel uncomfortable staying at the Mullinses' home without their approval.

Holly had tried at least two dozen times to reach her brother in the small Mexican village before she succeeded. Sometimes she felt so frustrated after unsuccessfully trying to place the call that she wanted to either fly down to Mexico to get permission or lie about having gotten it. But of course she couldn't spend money that wantonly or fib to Stephen. She knew her brother would whoop for joy at her having fallen in love and being loved in return by a man like Stephen. She knew also that neither Hank or Nettie would bat an eye at her having him stay for a weekend. Hank would think being asked for permission was quaint. Nettie would, too. But Stephen would not be budged; without the Mullinses' stated approval, he would not spend Friday through Sunday in their home.

Holly had accused him of having old-fashioned standards.

"Damned right," he had affirmed. "And values. I don't really want to spend a weekend with you. I want to spend a lifetime with you. Married." He said this while rubbing the small of her back.

"Okay, I can be ready in an hour," Holly had answered. It was Sunday, and they were at Stephen's house, using the afternoon wisely. He was lying on his back on the large white sofa and she was lying on top of him, luxuriating in the comfortable way her body fit against his. How clever of her body to have stopped growing when she was just this tall so she would fit on Stephen with her head resting on his wonderful chest and her toes wriggling against his.

But Stephen had not been willing to get up off the sofa and marry her in an hour. His old-fashioned values extended to wanting a real wedding, complete with Holly in a lovely white gown and their families standing behind them. That meant they would have to wait until Hank and Nettie returned from Mexico.

"We'd disappoint them if we didn't wait," he pointed out.

"Hank wouldn't mind. He's very easygoing," Holly protested.

"He very well may be, but he's a brother. He has a right to be looking on when his Gnat hooks up with another bug."

Holly groaned, but the groan was followed by three loving kisses against his chest and some very expressive toe wriggling. She was grateful that he cared about her brother's feelings.

Finally, Holly had been able to get through to Mexico, and both Hank and Nettie were jubilant about her new status of woman in love. Each managed to talk to Holly for two whole minutes about Stephen before asking how the babies were. At Stephen's insistence, Holly also asked permission for Gabriel to spend the weekend. Hank said, "Geez, I feel sorry for the poor thing. He never wanted to see a parrot again. Good thing there'll be a psychologist around."

Holly affectionately told her brother he was nuts, said goodbye, hung up the phone and flew into Stephen's arms. "Gabriel's invited to spend a weekend! And so are you!"

And tomorrow he was going to.

Today they couldn't see each other at all. Stephen was consulting at a large engineering firm in San Bernardino, and tonight, after dining with the firm's partners, he was seeing a new family of clients in his office.

But tomorrow would come like a gift for her and for Stephen. And like a headache for Gabriel.

AT LAST TOMORROW HAD become today. Holly moved through the early morning in a flurry of activity. At one point she supposed that if she'd been less happy, changing linen, vacuuming and dusting would not seem like a thrilling prelude to a working day. Nor would baking a pie. Stephen had mentioned once that he liked apple pie, and apple pie was what he would have tonight.

She wished she could stay home all day to prepare

nice things for tonight. But she had six lessons to give. That was really too many for one day, and she had made a mental note to space her sessions more carefully from now on. She would be on the road a lot today also, because two of the lessons—the first and the last, unfortunately—were in Rancho Mirage.

But she would have a two-hour break during the afternoon, and during that time she would buy a bouquet of flowers for the dining-room table and a gift to put under Stephen's pillow. Maybe a bottle of cologne or a pleasantly masculine soap on a rope. And of course she would buy groceries with which to make a memorable feast.

While putting the pearl-gray satin sheets on the bed, she thought that if she felt energetic at the end of the day she might whip up a cream of broccoli soup and that marvelous game hen recipe of Nettie's. Or maybe she'd go for a pair of succulent salmon steaks with an herb-butter sauce.

"Or," she mused to Alex, who was on the bird playpen Nettie and Hank kept on the dresser, "I might be lazy and grill hamburgers."

Alex squawked and Holly said, "Right. I'd better get back to work. First lesson is in an hour."

She finished making the bed and on surveying the finished product decided that a more beautiful bed had never existed. Would Stephen think she'd been silly to buy satin sheets? It had been a more costly indulgence than she was used to giving in to, by far.

No, she decided. She hadn't thought he was foolish two days ago when he gave her the outlandishly expensive perfume. It was a brand she had only seen previously in expensive ads, but there it was gift wrapped, with a card that said, "I love you. Stephen."

"You shouldn't have," she had said with a gasp while her eyes, very lingeringly, said thank you.

"Yes, I should have."

"I just meant that this is so costly. I've seen it advertised, but I didn't know people ever really bought it."

"People who are as conservative with their money as I am usually don't," he conceded while opening the tiny bottle.

Holly had swept her hair over one shoulder and tilted her head so he could touch a drop of the precious scent to the silken skin behind her ear.

"I won't spend money on lavish gifts like this very often," he murmured, dabbing the perfume on. The touch of his fingertip was followed by kisses behind, on and in front of her ear. "Only when I'm utterly unable to resist doing it. Do you think once a week would be too often?"

Holly had laughed as she took the bottle from him. She quickly replaced the stopper as if she was afraid that some of the perfume would be lost through evaporation.

And she had laughed again before kissing him. No, she had not thought him foolish for buying the legendary perfume. He would not think her foolish for buying satin sheets, or for having bought the plush terry kimono for him. It was hanging in the closet they would share this weekend, and it wasn't the only gift waiting for a houseguest. In her extravagant mood she had bought Gabriel a rubber mouse, even though he was probably too stoic a cat to be reduced to playing with toys.

She surveyed the sumptuous bed one last time and conceded wistfully that many hours would have to pass before she and Stephen got into it. But now it was time to dash to her first lesson. Lifting Alex from his playpen perch she left the bedroom. "It's into the cage for you, out of the oven for the pie and into the pool for me," she informed the bird cheerfully.

"I KNOW WHAT YOU'RE THINKING," the young woman sitting across from Stephen said after a long moment of silence. But she didn't go on.

"What am I thinking, Susan?" Stephen prompted. He felt very sorry for the young mother of two. She didn't have a black eye today. That had healed. But her marriage had not.

"That it's time for my marriage to come to an end?"

"All right. That's what I'm thinking. What are you thinking? Your thoughts on the subject are much more important than mine."

"That it's time for my marriage to come to an end," she said evenly, with conviction.

It really was. Stephen knew that it was even past time. It wasn't just that the poor woman was periodically struck by her irrational, jealous husband. It was that the man didn't want to change. He didn't want help. And when he wasn't being physically abusive to his wife, he abused her with words or neglect. Stephen cared about marriages and worked hard to help save them when there was something worth saving, but in this case there was nothing.

When the two o'clock session ended he felt dejected. He was relieved when the last client scheduled to see him called to cancel. It was Friday. He was going to Holly's for the weekend and didn't want to take any lingering gloom with him.

He wanted to take her flowers and a small gift. If he could finish all his chores early enough he'd have time to stop and buy her something. Nothing costly. He'd just given her perfume, and he didn't want her to start worrying that he couldn't hold on to a dollar.

Maybe something satiny for her to put on before bed, so he could take it right off. But did Holly go in for that stuff? He'd never seen her in a nightgown, come to think of it. Whenever they were between the sheets she was wrapped only in his loving arms. Sheets. He considered sheets. On the night Holly had forgotten to cover the birdcages and they had gone back to the Mullinses' house after midnight, he had slept over. There had been old faded sheets on the bed. One pillowcase even had a mended tear in it. Holly had laughed when she said that the Mullinses loved anything with a parrot motif so much they'd keep those sheets until they or the sheets died of old age.

That was it. He would buy sheets and surprise her with them. Satin sheets. More expensive than he'd intended, but oh, wouldn't it be worth it. He would find a way to keep her out of the bedroom for a while so he could remake the bed. Maybe he would run a bath for her, and while she was relaxing in it he would change the sheets.

He could picture her lying in her soft womanly loveliness between shimmery satin sheets. The top sheet would be pulled back to expose her breasts and navel. Her long golden hair would fan out over the pillow. And near her, beside the bed, flowers.

Roses. Yes, he would get roses and champagne and satin sheets. Tomorrow he would start being properly frugal.

Stephen felt much better than he had ten minutes before, and he was ready to get going. But while he'd been in the session with Susan he'd probably received a few calls. He would listen to the messages first, then pack what he would need for the weekend.

He turned the recorder on. The very first thing he heard was Holly's lovely voice calling him darling. She had phoned to tell him she couldn't wait for tonight.

Well, neither could he. When her message was over he listened for the next with some impatience, because he wanted to leave the office quickly.

"You seduced my wife, Dr. Gary. I am going to kill you."

Oh Lord! He had forgotten to call Bill Strand back. How long had it been since Bill's first nutty message? Stephen thought back to the evening Holly had become his lover and had entered this office to tell her story.

It was no wonder he'd forgotten. The memory of Bill's call had been overwhelmed by the emotional weight of that night. He flipped through his Rolodex and came to Bill's name. He paused before dialing the office number, to plan what he would say if he had to leave a message on Bill's recorder. Maybe just a terse, *Don't shoot!* No, he'd say, *You're too late, buddy. I've already died and gone to heaven.* Then he would give Holly's phone number. When Bill called him back at Holly's, he would say, "Here I am, in heaven. Just like I told you." It would not be an exaggeration.

He dialed Bill's office. A recorded message said that Bill would be back in the office on the first of the month.

Stephen frowned as he hung up and looked at the Rolodex card again to check Bill's home phone number. He dialed and a woman answered. It was Bill's mother. She explained that Bill and Nancy had gone to Europe for a whole month, and she was taking care of the children. Stephen asked when they had left for Europe. She told him. Stephen thanked her, said goodbye and hung up.

The caller had not been Bill. Stephen played the tape again and listened with extreme care. No, he did not know that voice. But if it wasn't Bill, it was not a joke.

If it wasn't a joke, it was a death threat. Stephen racked his brain. Who, who on God's earth, could be so benighted as to think that his wife had been seduced by Stephen Gary? He just could not come up with an answer. Maybe this was just the work of a prankster, some weirdo who got his jollies by shaking people up.

I'm probably taking it much too seriously, he thought, and he got up to leave the office. He would not let this day be ruined, because if it was ruined for him it would be ruined for Holly, too. He wasn't going to let that happen. She had looked forward to this weekend every bit as much as a child looks forward to Christmas morning. He turned out the light and locked up. Finished packing, Stephen set out to do his shopping. He knew of a store called the Bath and Bed Boutique. It was owned by friends of his parents.

What in blazes do I think I'm doing? he asked himself with a good measure of self-disgust after he'd turned the key in the ignition. If he went to Holly's tonight and some maniac followed him, Holly would be in extreme danger.

He got out of the car and went back to his office to get the recording, then he drove to the police department.

The detective with whom Stephen spent the next forty minutes did not think Stephen was taking the recorded messages much too seriously. He asked Stephen if any married woman he knew socially had acted flirtatiously toward him or might have a crush on him that could be perceived by her husband.

Stephen was able to honestly say no.

The detective asked Stephen if he could think of any client—any male half of a troubled marriage—that might think his wife was infatuated with him.

Stephen could not think of any.

Would Stephen mind letting the police tap his phone? And would he mind giving them a list of his married female clients?

Stephen said yes, emphatically, to both questions. He would mind. He explained briefly the importance of confidentiality in counseling.

The detective sighed and said he understood. "I used to get counseling when I was on the San Bernardino force," he told Stephen. "My therapist wouldn't have given my name out or let his phone be tapped, either."

They talked a while longer. The detective gave Stephen some fairly obvious advice, telling him to keep doors locked, make sure draperies were closed at night and to vary his jogging route.

"Do you have a security system?" the detective asked.

"Yes."

"A noisy dog?"

Stephen said no.

"I'd get a dog. And keep in touch. As a matter of fact I'd like to stop by your place tomorrow morning, first thing."

Stephen nodded. They shook hands again and Stephen left.

That was all Gabe needed, he thought as he got inside his car. To have to adjust to living with a dog after having spent a weekend with a bunch of parrots. Except that Gabe was not going to spend the weekend at the Mullinses' home. Not while this damned thing was going on. He wouldn't even think of subjecting Holly to any danger.

He sat in his car and thought about having to tell Holly that he wasn't coming for the weekend. He felt frustration rise in him until it had to be let out by banging his fist against the steering wheel and the dash. Damn! If some poor, disturbed soul had had to get it into his head that his wife was having an affair, why had he been selected as the likely lover?

Because you're a counselor and people fall in love with their counselors, he answered himself.

It was true. Many women fell in love with their male psychologists and many men fell in love with their female psychologists. Except that it wasn't really love. A good counselor got the client past the problem quickly, so that they could continue in a comfortable, professional, nonthreatening relationship. The "love" the client thought she felt wasn't love for him, but was love for someone else in her life.

But would the client's spouse realize that? If the spouse was a terribly troubled person who was not in therapy himself, might he not suspect an affair between his wife and her counselor? And might not that suspicion grow and grow until the jealousy it caused consumed him?

Stephen muttered an expletive and hit the steering wheel again, but this time he gave it a halfhearted slap. Oh hell. There was nothing he could do about this except protect the people he loved. Maybe the police would find the guy and relieve him of his murderous notions.

All he could do was put a little distance between himself and Holly and between himself and his parents. He wouldn't stop seeing them altogether; he couldn't explain a total absence. And they must not know about this. His parents would worry until they made themselves ill. And Holly...God only knew how the knowledge would affect Holly. She had already had a chunk of her life ruined when her closest friend was hurt by a sick person. He couldn't possibly tell her that he, whom she had grown to love, was now in harm's way.

How was he going to tell her? What would he tell her? He drove back home slowly, giving himself time to think of possible excuses for not spending the weekend at the Mullinses'.

When Stephen arrived home, Gabriel was on a leather ottoman in the den, watching as Stephen dialed Holly's number. "Don't look so relieved, dammit."

She answered the phone a little breathlessly after the fourth ring and told him in a cheery tone that it had taken her so long to answer because she'd been doing something very gourmet to two Cornish game hens.

He could picture the happiness in her sparkling blue eyes as she told him this. He could also picture how unhappy her eyes would look in one more minute. If he could have gotten his hands on the man who wanted to kill him, he would have strangled the bastard for changing the look in Holly's eyes.

"Holly, didn't you tell me that parrots are very susceptible to colds? That they can catch respiratory infections from humans?"

"Uh-huh. Why? Oh, Stephen, you don't...do you?"

"Yep. It just came on a few hours ago. I didn't call because I was hoping it was a false alarm. But it's definitely a cold."

"You don't sound like you have a cold."

"It's not in my nose yet. So far it's just in my throat. My throat's itching like crazy and I feel, you know, sort of rotten all over."

There was a pause, then Holly said, "That doesn't mean you can't be here. After all, Hank and Nettie must have colds once in a while. You'll just stay out of the family room."

"I don't think so, Holly. If they were our birds that would be one thing, but I don't think I can risk giving a cold to Hank and Nettie's babies."

There was another pause. Stephen knew how seriously Holly took her responsibility toward the birds. He was sure he'd won, that she wouldn't argue the fact that he could not come over tonight.

"I'll finish making our dinner and bring it over there," she said.

"No, don't do that."

"Why?"

"Because you'll catch the virus and then you'll give it to the birds."

"Stephen, are you saying that we aren't going to see each other until your cold is gone? That could be two weeks!"

He thought that two weeks might be enough time for the police to find out who wanted to kill him. But he couldn't do that to Holly. Not having an inkling of the real reason for his absence, she would feel abandoned.

"No, darling," he said, trying not to sound too morose. "I won't be as contagious as I am now in four or five days. Let's wait that long, just to be on the safe side. Okay?"

He had never heard "okay" said so sadly.

"I'll freeze the hens," she said. Then she told him she loved him. She sounded so deflated and so much like she was trying not to, that Stephen had to bite his lip. She told him to take aspirin every four hours and drink lots of liquids. She told him to get to sleep very early, and she would call him in the morning to see how he was feeling. She told him again that she loved him.

"I love you, my angel, more than you can possibly know." There was a feeling in his throat that could not be caused by any virus.

They hung up.

Stephen remembered the detective's advice: close all draperies at night. He went into the living room to do that. Pegasus stood in metallic beauty—a tribute to the myth-loving Greeks of yesterday and to an extremely talented artist of today.

Stephen remembered telling Holly, when she first saw and admired the sculpture, that he believed that something good could come from everything eventually.

What kind of good can come of this lousy situation, he asked the unperturbed sculpture.

None, he answered himself. *None whatsoever.*

11

"I THOUGHT YOU SAID the parrots talked." Linda peered at one exotic bird and then another. She had been in the family room with Holly for fifteen minutes and not one bird had said as much as hello to her.

"They do talk—most of them do. But never with a stranger around. They're very sensitive to anything new in their environment, especially people. If you came over often they'd talk when you were here. Daisy says she's 'in love and love is wonderful' every time I come into the house, unless I have someone she doesn't know with me."

Linda shrugged her shoulders and turned away from the birds. Looking at Holly she said, "Well, is Daisy right? Is love wonderful? I'm not a stranger to you. Are you going to talk to me about what's upsetting you?"

"It shows?" Holly asked. She hadn't said one word to Linda about how unhappy she felt.

"To someone who has known you as long as I have, it does. You were always too good at hiding your troubles, Hol. When we were young I admired you for it, especially when I was the one who had hurt you and you just took it on the chin and kept on smiling. But now I have a different perspective. I believe in putting problems out where they can be examined, not in impenetrable hiding places of the brain."

Linda lifted the shiny gold box that she had brought to Palm Springs off the sofa and set it on the cocktail table. "There, now I can sit next to you," she said, sitting down and looking directly at Holly. She waited.

Holly stared vacantly at the open box. Inside it was a flowing three-tiered, red-crepe evening dress with spaghetti straps and a plunging neckline. A soft maillot swimsuit was the surprise under the dress. Linda's mother had sent it to her but it hadn't fit, and rather than exchange it for something else, Linda had brought it to the desert this Friday evening to give it to Holly. She knew intuitively that it would not only fit her friend but would be stunning on her. What she had really come there for, though, was to meet the man who had made Holly so blissfully happy.

But Holly was as happy as a three-day-old tossed salad was fresh.

"Shoot," Linda ordered, when Holly continued to stare at the box and didn't say anything.

Holly obeyed, saying softly, "I hardly ever see him anymore."

"How long has this been going on?"

"A week."

"That's not so long," Linda suggested.

"Oh, yes it is. Two weeks ago, he wanted to see me every possible minute."

"Well, what happened?"

"If only I knew. He was supposed to spend last weekend here but he caught a cold, or at least he said he did. We didn't see each other at all for a few days, ostensibly because he was afraid of giving his virus to the birds."

"To the...these birds?" Linda looked incredulous.

"Yep. He thought we shouldn't see each other for five days, so he wouldn't be so contagious. Noble, wasn't he? But I couldn't wait that long, and I told him so after two days. He didn't seem sick then. Anyhow, he said he couldn't stay over this weekend because he was swamped with work. Besides counseling in his office he's doing a lot of consulting for businesses and he's revising some magazine articles that he's sold. So I couldn't argue with the fact that he has a lot to do, but I told him that being overworked doesn't mean you have to be alone. Then he said he felt we were rushing things, that we shouldn't chase romance out the window by being in each other's company twenty-four hours a day. Those were his words—the 'chasing romance out the window' part. I have to give him credit for saying it in a very loving way."

Linda made a face to show she was pondering the point, and then said that Stephen's reasoning was plausible. "Kevin and I are away from each other a lot," she told Holly. "We love each other like crazy, but we don't want to have each other underfoot, so to speak. There is something to be said for not being together too much. It sort of keeps the romance new and exciting."

"Maybe," Holly said, unconvinced.

"Having to part from each other is like the romance of the seashore, with the tide coming in and going out," Linda reflected. "I mean, if the tide just came in and stayed in it would lose some of its appeal, don't you think?"

Holly thought that if she and Linda lived to be a hundred, Linda would still be making her laugh. But just because she was laughing didn't mean she was happy. She was still miserable.

"What happens when you do see him?" Linda asked.

"Nothing unpleasant. We don't fight. He isn't cold. He's as sweet as ever, but... I don't know, Lin. He seems troubled. I really can't explain it."

"Try."

Holly tugged at the end of her braid, which was peeking over one shoulder, and thought of how to explain Stephen's behavior. She had showered just before Linda's arrival and had braided her hair afterward. The blue rubber band that had encircled this evening's newspaper held the braid in place.

"He always seems to want to meet in public and doesn't want to be alone with me anywhere," she began. "We've met at restaurants for lunch or dinner, and we went to a movie. But he doesn't want to come here, and he sure doesn't want me there. I drove over at night and he rushed me out of the house so fast you would have thought a woman was hiding in his closet or under the bed. He said he had a craving for ice cream, so we went to Häagen-Dazs. I'll tell you what he doesn't crave. He doesn't crave me."

"I don't know what to say," Linda said compassionately, "except that maybe you're imagining a change in his feelings for you. Maybe he caught a virus that wasn't noticeable to you but made him feel lousy, and maybe he's up to his ears in work. Period. Nothing to do with you."

"Maybe," Holly conceded. "And maybe not. I've been driving myself crazy trying to understand him. I thought there might have been another woman before I came on the scene, and he thought he was over her but isn't, and now he's seeing both of us while he decides. But I know Stephen wouldn't operate like that. He's mature and in control of his life, and he spends his life helping people—caring for them, not hurting them. Oh, I just don't know what to think, Linda. I'm angry with him. Damn but I'm angry with him. I want to shove him up against a wall and pin him there and scream 'Tell me what's gone wrong between us, you knuckleheaded cretin!'"

"You do?" Linda looked both dubious and impressed.

"You bet I do. And I also feel...I feel like I'm a plate of hotcakes that he's shoving one by one down the disposal."

"And I thought my 'tide coming in and going out' analogy was original," Linda mused.

"Well, I don't have to mope about it all night, not when you drove all the way from Laguna to see me and give me a beautiful dress."

Ignoring Holly's comment, Linda said, "I think he's scared."

"Of what?" Holly asked.

"Of exactly what he tried to tell you he was scared of. Of romance being chased out the window, of it becoming ho hum."

Holly didn't think so. Stephen seemed to want things to be ho hum now, instead of exciting. He was the one who had wanted to go to a movie; she would have rather stayed home to create their own love scenes. Last night, when he suggested they meet at Tony Roma's for dinner, she countersuggested that they eat at her place, so she could give him an appetizer, main course and dessert he would never forget. When they were finished with that she would have served him dinner. He'd said he didn't want her to have to cook. He wanted to take her out. Holly wouldn't beg or use anger to express her disappointment, so they went out. During dinner, while he told her about some of his consulting work, she remembered the joys of their beginning love, their passion. The splendid hours seemed so long ago, as long ago as a prior lifetime.

"He isn't acting like he's afraid of losing the romance, Lin. He's acting like it's already lost." Holly sighed and lifted a bare foot to the edge of the cocktail table. Her toe moved the gold box a fraction of an inch. Suddenly looking inspired, she practically bounced off the sofa. "Wait here!"

"Huh?"

Holly snatched up the box. "I'm going to get out of these jeans and into the dress. This gorgeous, slinky, seductive, sophisticated, man-killing dress that has a slinky, seductive bathing suit under it!"

"You're going to try to seduce him again, after he chose a sparerib dinner over your body?" Linda asked incredulously.

"Sure! Never say die!"

When she returned to the family room, Holly was wearing the one dress that had possibly, in a world filled with dresses, been created solely for the purpose of making Holly Hutton look bewitchingly feminine, seductive, romantic and classy. The effect was undermined somewhat, however, because her braided hair was still restrained by blue rubber.

A small folded card was attached to one spaghetti strap of the dress. It lay half-open and propped against Holly's breast. On the outside of it was the Italian designer's name. On the inside was written, "Dance all night in the Mermaid's Delight."

"Oh! You look gorgeous!"

"Let's hope so, because I'm going over to Stephen's. And if he doesn't... if he won't... I'll...."

"What?" Linda prodded.

"I'll take the dress off, strangle him with it and come back here wearing the bathing suit."

"You've got that much guts?" Linda asked, getting up from the sofa.

"I do!"

"Then get me a pair of scissors."

"Huh...?"

"Holly, you look sensational. But the braid has got to go."

"I can't believe we're doing this. Are you sure?"

Holly was sitting on a stool in the dressing room, facing the mirror over the vanity. Linda had spread newspapers on the floor and a beach towel was draped over Holly's shoulders to protect the new dress from falling hair. "The last time you cut my hair we were in the fifth grade. My mother was not happy with the results," Holly recalled.

"I've gotten better. Honest. Trust me. I always cut my own hair, and I've cut Kevin's. Jewelry makers are natural hairstylists. Just relax and think of yourself as a vamp. Vamps don't wear braids. Think of the look on Stephen's face when he sees the all-new exciting Holly Hutton. She's dazzling, she's dramatic, she's...."

Linda made the first cut.

"STEPHEN...."

"Holly...?"

"In here. Don't turn the light on, please."

While driving, Holly had lost most of her anger and some of her nerve. But despite a growing belief that what she was doing would backfire on her, she used the house key Stephen had given her and entered his home. Once inside, though, she didn't know what to do with herself. He could be gone for hours, maybe the whole night. Her options for action, as she stood in his entry hall dressed to entice and seduce, seemed limited to finding something to read or watching television.

Instead she had impulsively climbed up on Pegasus. One minute later she heard the garage door open and the sound of the door between the garage and service porch, then Stephen's steps as he walked through the house. Her heartbeat had quickened and for a painful moment she wanted to jump down and run away—to escape the possibility of rejection. Rejection was, she felt deeply, a strong possibility.

Stephen walked into the living room. He did not put a light on.

"I wanted to climb up on this thing from the moment I first saw it," Holly said with a nervous laugh. "I guess I'm still a tomboy at heart."

"Yes, well... let me help you down. You could fall."

"No! I don't want to get down! I once thought that you had put me on a pedestal, Stephen, and that scared me a little because if you're on a pedestal you're likely to fall off it. But then I thought, if I fell you would catch me, so I wasn't worried. And I'm not worried about falling off Pegasus. I don't want to get down yet."

Actually, her hold on the horse was precarious and she was uncomfortable. The metal was cold against her skin.

"I'll put a light on."

"No! Please don't! I opened the draperies so I'd have the light from outside, but I don't want you to turn any lamps on in here."

She didn't want him to see her because she knew that he wouldn't like her hair. It was in a blunt cut, ending at her jawline. The bangs covered her forehead entirely. Except for when she moved her head suddenly—causing the bangs to separate—they covered her eyebrows and created a bold frame for her eyes.

After cutting Holly's hair, Linda had made up her face. The result was a more provocative and dramatic-looking woman than Holly had ever appeared before. But that woman's heart was breaking, and her eyes had the smudged look of a child who has been betrayed by a trusted friend.

"Holly, I have to close the draperies. Then I'll have to put a light on, because I am afraid of your falling even if you're not."

"Why do you have to close them?" she asked quickly to stall for time.

"I just do."

"Are you afraid someone will come by and see me in here?" *A woman? One you're expecting,* she added silently.

Stephen didn't answer the question Holly had asked out loud, but crossed the room to close the curtains. Then he turned a lamp on. The light was soft but effective. He could see her clearly.

"My God," he murmured, looking with fierce intensity at Holly.

She turned her face from him, resting her burning cheek on the cool metal mane of the sculpture.

"Look at me," Stephen ordered.

Holly did, and seeing a fierceness she perceived to be anger in his gaze, she changed her attitude about this confrontation. Who was he to judge her? She would not be afraid of him. What could he do if he didn't like the way she looked? Hurt her? Reject her? It had been so thoroughly done during the past week that anything else he did would be anticlimactic.

"You . . . ." Stephen stopped after the one word and came closer to her.

Fierceness blazed from Holly's own eyes as she said, "I may as well get down now." She managed in one deft movement to be sitting on Pegasus as if she was riding sidesaddle on a living horse. Then, before Stephen could reach out to help her, she slipped down the sculpture's smoothly rounded side and to the floor. She landed on her bare feet without hurting herself.

"Holly, you should have let me help you! You . . . ." He gripped her bare arms. Without finishing what he had intended to say he surveyed Linda's artistry. His eyes narrowed and the muscles of his jaw were tight.

"Don't you like it, Stephen?" Holly asked in what she hoped was a taunting tone. "I do! I—"

His mouth came down over hers so crushingly it could have been a punishment, but for Holly the punishment had ended. She accepted the kiss as a gift and moaned in her hunger for him. Stephen's tongue quickly informed her of his own need, and the passionate force of his touch drove home the point. Wherever his hands roved roughly, Holly's skin felt her love-fired blood rush to the surface. When the kiss was done and the fierce caresses abated, Stephen held her head back with his strong hands and then lifted her hair in fistfuls. He let go of it, allowing it to fall in symmetrical sheets against the sides of her face.

"It will grow back," Holly said weakly.

"It's beautiful," he whispered hoarsely. "It frightens me to have you look so beautiful. That dress, your hair, the way you're made up. Holly, how will I be able to keep other men away from you if you look like this?"

"Easily, if you want to. Do you want to?"

"Do you have to ask?" His voice was husky, and his hands moved from her hair to the sides of her bare throat, then down over the softness above the deep vee of the dress. When his hands found her breasts they stopped.

"Stephen," Holly breathed, as her hands moved slowly along the muscular arms that would enfold her as she slept tonight, "the designer knew that I would be wearing this dress."

Stephen's hands went slowly around Holly's waist. His eyes looked into hers as if he was entranced by the mysteries he saw hidden there. "How do you know that?"

"There's a bathing suit under it. And the tag said it was for dancing all night. Do you want to dance with me?"

"Yes, beautiful mermaid. I'll take you dancing."

"No, don't take me dancing. Dance with me here. Please."

For a moment he looked unyielding, and Holly thought he was going to maneuver her out of the house quickly as he had on the night they went to the ice-cream parlor. But when she lifted her arms to put them around his neck his look softened. Then he molded his body lightly against hers.

Without music, without moving except ever so slightly, they danced. For Holly, the dance was an expression of her love for Stephen. But all too soon he released her, stepped away and put his hands behind his back.

Holly was looking up at the face she adored, but she felt no peace. The music inside her heart had stopped. Stephen's withdrawal had ended it. The silence was deafening.

"Is the band taking a break?" she asked with a hollow laugh.

"It is. It isn't a very good band anyway. Let's go someplace where the music is better. I know a place that's—"

"No! I don't want to dance anymore!" Holly lifted her chin defiantly, trying desperately to salvage her pride and keep from crying. "I know!" she cried almost frantically. "Let's swim!" She reached behind her back to undo the dress.

Stephen shook his head slightly and said no softly.

"Why not?" Holly demanded. "It'll be chilly in the pool, but you're not afraid of a little cold, are you Stephen?"

Resentment had put an icy edge on her words; she knew it but didn't care. She gazed steadily up at him in anticipation of a suggestion that they go swimming at a hotel pool. If he dared do that she was going to turn and walk out of the house.

"We can't swim now. I put chlorine in the pool just a while ago, right before I came inside. I'd meant to do it this afternoon but forgot."

Holly stared at her bare feet. She couldn't look

him in the eyes for a moment, because there were hot tears of shame in her own. She was ashamed for Stephen, for his being reduced to lying to her, and for herself because she still loved him, still needed him.

The disappointment she felt didn't diminish her love. The hurt and rage welling up in her didn't lessen it. Her desire was so great she felt herself on the verge of sinking to her knees. Once before she had been on her knees before Stephen and had begged him to yield to her desire, and he had.

But that had been different. He had been in love with her then. She had just heard him shout it out to a lizard. She thought wryly that the thing he'd neglected to tell his reptilian confidant was that for Stephen Gary love was temporary.

She would not get down on her knees. She would continue to love him and ache for him, but she would do it standing up, and proud.

"Holly, let's go somewhere."

Quickly and coolly, betraying no pain with her voice, she said, "That's okay, Stephen. We don't have to go anywhere together. I heard you get out of your car inside the garage and come right into the house, by the way. Goodbye."

She began to walk from the room.

"Wait."

She stopped and turned.

"You forgot your shoes." He picked the high-heeled strappy sandals up, but didn't hold them out for her to take. Instead he held them behind his back. "I don't want you to go, darling. I know I've made you upset and angry, but Holly, there are things you don't understand."

She walked right up to him and asked, "Well, would you like to explain them to me?"

"No—for your sake, no. I wish you would just trust me, and have faith in me."

"Okay. I trust you and have faith in you. Will you do something for me in return?" She blinked away tears with the question, but she needn't have bothered because more appeared to take their place.

"I hope you're going to ask me to love you, Holly. Because I already do and always will."

"That's not it. I want to stay here all night. Stephen, will you let me stay the night with you?"

"You have to cover the birdcages," he reminded her. "If you don't go home and do that the babies will all have neuroses." He attempted a laugh, but it was mirthless.

"Linda's there. She'll cover them."

Stephen sighed.

Holly knew a sigh that meant no when she heard one. "Give me my shoes," she whispered.

He did, and she left.

12

STEPHEN PROWLED THE LIVING ROOM, walking back and forth in front of the metal sculpture without looking at it. He knew that if he looked up at the arched back and neck he would see a vision of Holly there; her red dress draping her thighs voluptuously, her slender bare feet dangling against the horse's sides.

He paced, pounding a fist repeatedly against the palm of his other hand. How he had wanted to tell her the truth! He had longed to reassure her of his love, to banish forever the feeling of rejection that was crushing her.

Her feeling of rejection came through in her voice, in her look when she gazed searchingly into his eyes, and even in her gestures and walk. She had come to him as beautiful as a Greek goddess and had climbed proudly onto Pegasus as if the superb sculpture were her throne. Still, the rejection she was feeling had shown through.

He had wanted to tell her that she had no cause to feel unloved, that to the contrary his love for her had been growing every day—even on the days when he didn't see her. On those days love was nurtured by the loneliness he felt for her, and by the flood of memories of their shared moments.

He had wanted to answer all the tormented questions in her eyes with one truth: *I love you, Holly.* When she asked him if she could spend the night, he had yearned to answer by lifting her and carrying her to his bed.

But there was another part of him that feared putting Holly in danger, and feared what knowing about the death threats might do to her. That part guided him to protect her, then left him to sit helplessly back and watch her feel hurt.

The double bind was eating him up. Even now, he was torn between wanting to go after her to tell her the truth and wanting to stay here to protect her from possible harm and certain mental anguish.

At last he wearied of pacing and sat down. He stared at Pegasus while brooding on his options. Staring at the mythical horse, he was reminded of the morning he and Holly had gone horseback riding. Before the dawn ride he had fantasized watching Holly from behind as her bottom bounced seductively on the saddle, her hair bouncing in the same tantalizing rhythm against her back. So much had changed since the time of that fantasy. The first change was in his attitude. When they were actually astride the horses he had not wanted to ride behind her, to watch her from that vantage point as if crudely surveying a plaything that existed only to amuse him. He had wanted to ride beside her because she was his equal in dignity. And that was what he had done.

That was the first change. It had occurred to him then that he was certain of his love for her and that they would share a good life. The second change was in Holly. She had lost all fear of being in love and being his lover.

The third change was that someone had robbed their life of goodness. After the first two death threats there had been several more, not only by phone but in the mail.

The fourth change to occur after the morning of their dawn ride over the desert, he mused as he stood up, was that Holly's beautiful long hair was now shorter. He liked it. There was only one change among these four that was negative, but its impact was overwhelming. So he was going to do something about it now.

The police were doing their part, what little they could. They patrolled the house frequently, especially at night. Stephen sometimes worried that the surveillance of his property could wind up being an intrusion on his clients' privacy, but he was practical enough to know he must allow it.

Some things he would not allow, though. The detective who was working on this case had suggested that Stephen leave the premises at night, so he could stay in the house in his place. Stephen would not consider it; he would not let another man put his life on the line for him.

"It's my job, pal," the detective had said laconically.

Stephen hadn't given in. The detective had shaken his head and said, "You're just like my therapist in San Bernardino. You people spend all your time worrying about the welfare of others and don't think about yourselves."

Not true. Stephen did think about himself. He didn't want anything to happen to him because he loved life. He wanted lots and lots of life to be left to him, so he could spend all of it with Holly.

For a week he had hardly spent any time with her because somebody neither of them knew had decided to have life-and-death power—or at least the power of terrorism—over him. It was insanity. It was not going to go on. He would go to Holly tonight, tell her the truth, and assure her that he would find a way to be with her. They could stay in a hotel or spend weekends out of town.

But that would be insanity, too, he reflected. He couldn't become a hunted nomad, dragging Holly along with him.

Stephen whirled in a sudden eruption of rage and drew his arm back to take a poke at Pegasus. He stopped himself just in time. A broken hand was not something he needed.

He got inside his car and used the automatic garage door control that was lying on the seat next to him. As he backed the Firebird out of the garage he looked around to make sure he wasn't being followed. He didn't want to take any chances, didn't want to lead the would-be assassin to Holly's.

Realizing how wound up he was, he turned on the car radio, thinking that music would lighten his mood. Even though he was going to tell Holly the truth, he wanted to be able to reassure her, to sugarcoat the pill a little. If he wasn't calm and in complete control of his emotions, he wouldn't be able to do that. The song that Julio Iglesias had been singing came to an end and there was a newsbreak. When Stephen heard, "Crime statistics have taken a turn for the ..." he switched the radio off.

"I don't want to hear it."

He remembered that Linda was at the house with Holly. That was good. Holly's having an old friend with her when she heard what he had to say might be a comfort. He assumed that Holly and Linda had been through so much together they must be exceptionally good at giving each other moral support.

He hoped so.

Stephen looked around once more when he pulled into the Mullinses' driveway. He thought that if he lived to be very old he would not want to have to do anything as unpleasant and demeaning as this again. Looking over his shoulder for danger made him feel less free.

Holly wasn't home.

When Stephen rang the bell, Linda took a long while to get to the door, then asked in a sleepy voice, "Who is it?" Stephen told her and she unlocked the door quickly. Before he could say a word, Linda asked, "Where's Holly? What's happened?"

"Nothing's happened, Linda. Don't be alarmed," Stephen said, although he was alarmed himself. He didn't like the idea of Holly being out in her car when she was so upset. But to allay Linda's concern he said, "I just thought Holly would be home by now. She left my house a few minutes before I did."

"When was that? Why did she leave? Was she okay?"

Linda asked the three questions in a rush of words, and Stephen could tell that she was as worried about where Holly was as he.

"Look, I'm sure there's nothing to worry about. She must have stopped somewhere. At a market or drugstore. Before she left here, did she mention that she needed anything?" he asked.

"You."

Linda's abrupt honesty and timing had been so perfect that in other circumstances Stephen would have laughed. He didn't even smile. "I know that," he said softly. "Was there anything else, so I'll have an idea where to look for her?"

"Uh uh. Do you want to come in and wait?"

He considered it. Holly might have stopped to get something or she could be driving around awhile to settle her nerves before coming home to Linda's personal questions. But he didn't really think so. There was another possibility—a place where she could be—that had just occurred to him. He wanted to get there so badly he regretted the time it took to say, "No thanks. Linda, don't worry. Holly is all right. You don't have to wait up for her, and don't feel concerned if she doesn't come home tonight. She probably won't."

He ran the few steps to his car and backed into the street while Linda stood under the porch light, watching him. He saw her raise her hand and expected her to wave. Instead she made a thumbs-up sign.

He was sure now that Holly had gone to the canyon. It took as much restraint as he was able to muster to drive there at a reasonable rate of speed. He wanted to push the accelerator right through the car floor. He didn't. It seemed like an eternity, but at last he came to the spot where Holly would have pulled off the road.

Yes. He could see the car. It was alone in the dark, as if abandoned.

As he pulled closer, Stephen felt angry with Holly for the very first time. How dare she walk out across the desert and into the canyon alone at night? Didn't she have any sense? He felt like thrashing her, at least verbally.

Okay, Stephen, forget it, he told himself. *She came here because she's sick at heart. She doesn't need to be told off, she needs to be told she's loved.*

Then, as he opened the door of his car, he could see that she hadn't walked out across the desert. She was sitting in her car. For a woman to sit alone in a car on a deserted road at night was dangerous enough, but he wouldn't mention it when he got inside with her.

When he was standing beside her car he was relieved to see that the doors were locked. At least she had taken that precaution. He leaned down to talk to her as she rolled the window down.

"Holly . . . ."

"Please go away, Stephen. I came here to be by myself."

"Honey, I'm sorry. I didn't mean—"

She rolled the window up.

He tapped on the window, gently. A moment later he tapped again, less gently.

She didn't budge.

Damn. He wished the doors weren't locked. He started to talk to her through the window, which meant he had to shout. It made him feel ridiculous. "You're acting like a child!" he yelled. "Will you please open the door."

No response.

He shoved his hands into his pockets and turned his back to the car. *Don't get angry,* he told himself. *She doesn't need you to be angry with her.*

He turned and leaned down again. "Holly, I just want to talk to you!"

She rolled the window down. "I asked you to go away. I want solitude. When you've wanted to be alone I've tried to respect your wishes. Please respect mine."

"But—"

She rolled the window up. He pounded his fist on the top of the car, then kicked a tire. He tried again, shouting, "Holly, I know how angry you are, but you're defeating the purpose of having come here! You came here hoping I'd find you! Now I've found you, like you wanted, so open the door!"

No response.

Being a man who didn't go in for shouting at people, Stephen felt like an ass. He also felt angry. *Holly, if I was as strong as I'd like to be right now, I'd lift the car and turn it over. Then you'd open the door.*

But his many hours of weight lifting hadn't brought him to that point. He couldn't turn the car over or talk sense into Holly; nor could he see any purpose in standing outside her car while she sat in there. He walked back to his own car and got inside. But he didn't start the engine. There was no way he was going to leave his beloved, stubborn, unreasonable, unmovable, angry Holly out on the highway in a locked car. He would just sit and watch her until she got tired of being watched and drove home.

The door on the passenger side of Holly's car swung open.

Stephen got out of his own car and walked to Holly's. "Hi," he said, getting in.

Holly didn't answer him. There would have been no sound at all in the car, but Stephen's foot struck something on the floor. He looked down at what appeared to be an unopened bottle of wine. She *had* stopped to buy something.

He wanted to reach out and touch her; he especially wanted to touch her hair. But then he thought better of it. Her head was bent forward so that the blunt line of her hair obscured most of her profile. He still was not used to her new look. The haircut had obviously been an attempt to create a sophisticated look, and in a way it did. But it also made her appear more exposed, and that vulnerability made him want desperately to touch her.

She still hadn't spoken, so Stephen got right to the heart of the matter. "Holly, I love you. I know I've been hurting you, and I'm sorry."

She turned to face him. His heart wrenched. If a woman made her face up to look worldy, she shouldn't sit in a car and cry. Holly's tears had dried, but even in the half-light dark rings of mascara showed beneath her eyes and the makeup on her cheeks looked streaked.

He touched a finger tenderly to a mascara smudge, then whispered, "Come here."

She did. She yielded, and he took her into his arms with such enormous relief that he momentarily forgot the cause of their misery. But then he remembered. He would tell her now while he held her close, so that at the moment she first felt the fear she would be able to cling to him.

"Holly, I have to tell you why I've been acting the way I have."

"No," she said. The word and a simultaneous sniffle were muffled against his shoulder. "If it's about another woman, I don't want to hear about it. And if it's because of your work, I don't want to know."

He released his hold on her so he could look into her eyes. "Another woman? Darling you know there isn't any other woman." He stroked her hair, then laid his hand gently against her face. "It does have something to do with my being a psychologist."

"I thought that was it."

"What did you think?" He opened the glove compartment to get another Kleenex.

Holly used the tissue, then told him what she had determined. She had decided, while sitting there, that he was used to helping troubled people get back on their feet. When they no longer needed him he sent them on their way so they could get on with leading their lives.

Stephen looked at her in much the same way she

had looked at him when he'd told her his favorite flavor of ice cream was hotcakes. "You don't really believe that," he insisted finally.

"I didn't want to think it was another woman that had come between us. Something came between us—something or someone—and I just didn't want it to be a woman. I thought there might have been someone you'd been seeing before we met, and that she had come back into your life. I thought you might be struggling with making a choice. Dammit to hell, Stephen, what was I supposed to think? That you had a cold and lots of work to catch up on? What would you have thought if it had been the other way around, and I was the one who avoided being alone with you?"

Stephen sighed. He swallowed hard, then said, "Someone did come between us, but not a woman. It's a man."

"Very funny." She glared at him.

"No, it's not. It's not funny at all. Holly...." He stopped, wishing with all his heart that he could leave the words unsaid. But there was no backing down now. "Holly, let me hold you while I tell you what's come between us." He reached for her, but this time she didn't come into his arms.

"No. Just tell me. Tell me how your being a psychologist has something to do with it, and how a man has something to do with it. I thought I didn't want to know before, but now I'm dying to. I want to know what could possibly justify your destroying our relationship."

"A man wants to kill me."

13

HOLLY LAUGHED, but it was a hollow and abrupt sound. What craziness was Stephen talking about? Why would he say such a thing to her?

He reached out to hold her again, and she pushed him back forcefully with both hands. She shook her head to let him know that she wasn't going to tolerate such nonsense. Kill him? Why would anyone want to do that? No. No! She was not going to hear any more of this absurdity. Stephen was beginning to talk again so she put her hands over his mouth. "Stop! You're crazy! It's not true!"

He pulled her hands away and held them against his chest. Holly could feel his heartbeat. A flash of a sweet memory—the desert picnic, Stephen holding her hand against his chest—stabbed at her. His heartbeat flowed into her hand and joined with her own. And now he was telling her that the beat of his heart might be stilled. She wanted to scream at him some more, to scream her denial until she was hoarse and couldn't go on. But terror froze her voice. She sat in numb silence now, with no choice except to hear what Stephen had decided to tell her.

"A man thinks his wife is having, or had, an affair with me, and his jealousy has caused him to slip into a

. He leaves death threats on my answering aily and he's also sent threats in the mail."

When he stopped talking she got as deeply inside his embrace as the front seat of the car would allow. He told her it was going to be all right, that nothing would happen to him. She whispered his name over and over again, then said, "Stephen, we'll go away. We'll go away together tomorrow. No, we'll leave tonight! We'll just disappear and he won't be able to find you! We won't come back here! We'll—"

"Holly, hush a minute. Just be still."

He was caressing the back of her neck and murmuring reassurances. She was struck by compassion, wishing Stephen had not endured the past week without her support. Oh, why hadn't he told her? She realized that he had been trying to protect her from physical harm and spare her anguish. But she wished so much that he hadn't. He had needed her and she hadn't been there. But she could help him now, and would.

"It will be all right," she said in a tone of fierce conviction. "We can go to stay with my brother. You'll be safe there, and we won't have to be apart. I'm calm now, Stephen, and rational. You have to agree with me that it's the best thing to do. Come away from here with me right away. Please. Actually, I've longed for you to meet Hank and Nettie. We'll just use this as an excuse to visit them."

As she spoke she explored his face with one hand, bringing her fingers to his lips when she uttered the final plea. She wanted to feel as well as hear him say that he would get away.

Stephen kissed her fingers, but didn't say what she wanted to hear. "Your fingers taste like salt. Were you wiping tears away with them?"

She nodded. As she'd been driving and then when she was sitting alone in the car, she had wiped tears away again and again until she finally gave up and just let them flow. He kissed her fingers once more, then touched them to his chin. "Remember when you touched my chin during the picnic? It drove me wild. I'll never forget that."

Holly remembered. It made her start crying again. "Thanks," she whispered when he handed her a tissue. She blew her nose, then listened as Stephen related the whole story. He said that the detective on the case was confident that it would be solved soon. He told her he had been avoiding his parents, and that when Holly gave Mary her swimming lesson she must be careful not to reveal anxiety. He ended by saying that Palm Springs was his home and nobody was going to chase him away from it. He mentioned also that he had clients who needed him.

"You could take a vacation. Everyone takes vacations, even counselors."

"I just had a vacation," he reminded her. "I spent two weeks fishing and caught a mermaid."

She knew he was trying to make her smile, and then she was struck by the thought that he might really need just that from her. She wasn't the only one in this car who wanted solace. So she tried hard and smiled.

He smiled back. "I love you so much," he said, brushing his lips softly over hers. The smiles were gone now, but they had had an effect. Holly felt a little better.

"Oh, honey, this was such a lousy week. It feels so good to be with you—really with you—again," Stephen murmured.

"Stephen, what are we going to do?" She asked it calmly even though she knew the answer was not going to be that they were flying to Mexico.

"We're going to wait it out. We're also going to cooperate with the police and with each other. That means I'm going to find ways to see you more, but I won't put you in danger. And you're going to help by understanding that I can't spend the night in your home, and you can't spend the night in mine."

"I understand," Holly said. Then she was sobbing again and he held her very tight.

When she was through he wiped the tears away and warned, "Better not cry anymore. We're at the bottom of the package."

"I've been blubbering so much tonight I don't know if I can keep from starting again, but I'll try. Does the color of my nose match my dress?"

He tilted her head back. "It's hard to tell in here. Let me put the light on." He flicked the car ceiling light on and studied the situation. "It doesn't quite match, but it's such a lovely shade of pink I have to—" He stopped talking and turned the light off, simultaneously kissing the tip of her nose. When they moved to embrace his foot touched the bottle on the floor and it rolled. He reached down to pick it up, asking, "What is this? Wine?"

"Sparkling apple cider. I stopped at a liquor store when I left your house. I thought I'd bring champagne to our canyon and celebrate having had the courage to walk out on you. I didn't want to leave you. I wanted to get down on my knees and beg. Anyhow, I bought cider instead of champagne."

"Couldn't drink alone?" he asked gently, putting the bottle back down.

Holly gazed at him a long moment before quietly saying, "I couldn't drink at all, not under any circumstances."

Stephen gave her a questioning look. On several occasions they had had wine with dinner.

"I'll explain later," Holly said. "Stephen, I want something. I want it very much."

"I don't think I could refuse you anything, not tonight."

"Then be prepared to sleep under the stars tonight, darling. I want to spend the whole night in the canyon, where our descendants are going to conduct tours of our love shrine."

He looked doubtful, and tracing the curve of one red spaghetti strap over her shoulder he said, "It's too cold for you to spend the night outdoors, Holly, especially wearing a skimpy evening dress."

"Stephen, it's about seventy degrees right now," she said softly. "I won't be cold, but if I am you'll hold me tighter."

"You could wear my jacket," he said thoughtfully.

A victory smile began to play on her lips. "And you've got that big blanket in the trunk of your car, the one we picnicked on. I've got a flashlight and a bottle of cider. That's all we need. Come on." She reached for her door handle.

"Are you sure? It's a crazy idea, Holly. I want to take good care of you from now on. You shouldn't have climbed up on Pegasus, by the way."

"Please start taking good care of me by sleeping all night with me in the desert. And if you make love to me first, I'll give you a reward."

"What's the reward?"

"First, I'll tell you why I bought the cider instead of champagne. Second, I'll stay off of Pegasus."

It was obviously an offer he couldn't refuse. She grinned as he reached for his door handle.

Holly began to undress. Stephen, in a cautioning tone, said, "I hope you know what you're getting yourself into. It's not too late to back out. I would understand."

Holly laughed and looked at him quizzically. "Why would I want to back out? This is what I've longed for for a week."

He moved very close to her, close enough for his chest to excite her nipples to taut arousal, close enough to make her thighs tingle with awareness of his masculine power. But he did not embrace her. As if meaning to tease her, he kept his hands at his sides; he nuzzled her face but volunteered nothing more. To Holly this was like being made to stand two steps back from a richly laden banquet, starving and nibbling a saltine. She put her hands over his and drew them upward so she could place them on her breasts. "Why would I back out?" she asked again, gazing up at him with undisguised desire. "It's been a long time, or so it seems."

"That's the point," Stephen replied as he began to tease her nipples with thumb-tip caresses. The sensations of these tender touches on her breasts made Holly gasp. She uttered a soft sound that was half a hungry moan, half a satisfied purr.

Stephen chuckled and continued his playful stroking. "It's been so long that there's a lot of loving to make up for," he said. Then he grazed his lips over hers lightly, as lightly as his thumbs were toying with her nipples. Holly's lips parted in an attempt to turn his teasing kiss into a passionate one, but Stephen moved his mouth away from hers. His lips grazed over her cheek and came to rest near her ear. "Once you're out of this beautiful dress...." He paused, and his tongue flicked inside her ear. "It is all going to happen."

"The dress has a bathing suit under it, remember?" Holly said on the end of a deep sigh. "Tell me what will happen when I get out of the beautiful dress and the beautiful bathing suit."

He dipped his head down so he could kiss the soft hollow at the base of her throat. Holly's head was tilted back; her face was to the stars. Her legs were not strong enough to hold her now. Stephen seemed to know what was happening inside her; he supported her tightly with his hard-muscled arms. But he continued to titillate her.

"What will happen, beautiful mermaid lady, is that I will order you to undress me." He paused again, this time to kiss her below the bare clavicle, then went on, "While you're innocently removing my jacket and shirt and belt and pants, you will know that all the lovemaking I've been wanting to lavish on you for many nights—and mornings—is going to be unleashed on you in one incredible night."

Holly breathed deeply. She was almost unable to speak. But she managed to whisper while Stephen once again seared her ear with his tongue, that when a woman removes a man's clothes in the desert at night she is not removing them innocently. "I've been as starved as you have for just as many nights," she warned him. Her hands left their hold on the back of his neck and raked forcibly through his hair for emphasis.

He didn't answer. Keeping one arm around her, he lifted the softly flowing skirt of her dress and draped it over his arm, then felt for the close-fitting material of the bathing suit. While the sleek fabric between her burning thighs was a barrier to Stephen's exploring fingers, it couldn't prevent the sensations from penetrating and flooding Holly with increased desire. He continued the slow, maddening strokes, first tracing the curves where fabric ended and silken flesh began, then gliding back and forth along the center of the material.

"Stephen..." Holly managed to gasp.

"Mmm."

"Please...let me get out of the beautiful dress... and bathing suit...now."

"You're sure? There are nights and mornings and even afternoons to make up for. Once you're undressed, my angel, I don't know if I could let you back out of any of our missed lovemaking."

Holly thought that if she wasn't released from his hold on her so she could remove her clothes calmly, she would end up tearing them from her body. She withdrew her hands from the thick dark hair she loved so much, brought them down to his magnificent shoulders, and then placed them on his steel-muscled upper arms. "Stephen...I'm beginning to think...."

She stopped. She could think, but it was hard to talk because Stephen's finger was still enjoying its private rendezvous with the bathing-suit fabric between her thighs. She finally blurted out, "I'm beginning to think you're the one who might back out! You're afraid that I'll ravish you!"

He let her go, grinned and stepped well back from her. Placing his hands at his waist he said, "I accept the challenge. Undress."

When she was naked she undressed Stephen completely, as he had said that she would. And, as she had predicted, she didn't feel innocent while performing this task. As each part of his exquisite body gleamed nude beneath the stars, Holly fantasized pressing her lips to it, licking it with the moist tip of her tongue and nipping at it with her teeth. She did none of this while she undressed him, though, and he in turn allowed her body respite from his explorations.

But Holly quivered with the sure knowledge of what was to follow. When she knelt to slide his briefs down and his manhood surged upward in its new freedom, she was so overcome by desire she could not have stood back up.

She stayed on her knees on the white blanket. Resisting the urge to bestow a kiss on what would soon be buried deep within her, she began to tease Stephen's body as he had teased hers. She touched her lips to the outside of his powerful thigh and then kissed him—sometimes with petal-soft brushes of her lips, sometimes with flicks of her tongue—all the way down his leg. She encircled the prominent bone of his ankle with her smoothly gliding tongue, and then grazed her lips around his foot so she could begin the tantalizing kisses upward.

To be able to bend all the way forward and kiss his ankle and feet, Holly had had to move back on her knees, so when Stephen bent down and cupped his hand over her head he was leaning above the long arc of her spine. "Stop," he ordered.

"Why, darling?" After the question she kissed his foot again.

"It's too much. It's driving me wild."

"You can take it," she murmured.

"Holly, it's torment. I want you so badly. Rockets are going off."

"Let them go off." She laughed softly. "We'll keep lighting more. I can't believe that the man who wants to give me a whole week of love in one night won't let me make up for a little lost time myself."

He sighed and released her head. He straightened and dug his toes into the soft blanket. "Your logic is always faultless," he said. "Go ahead, then. I'm on fire and I'm yours. Make up for lost time."

She did; then she lay down on the blanket. Stephen towered over her for a moment, and she had the joy of looking at him and the universe's gift of stars both at once. "Aren't you going to come down here with me?" she asked playfully.

"Oh, I am. I was just deciding which night of deprivation I wanted to make up for first. I think...." He got down on his knees, astride her. "I think we'll go all the way back to when I was supposed to come to your place but pretended to have a cold." He looked in mock seriousness at her and asked, "Would you rather I put last Friday on hold, and start off with Saturday morning? Saturday morning is going to be a real winner."

Holly moved in voluptuous anticipation beneath him. "Friday," she murmured. "Let's not skip around. We'll do this in chronological order. And you just wait, Dr. Gary, until you find out what I had planned for that Friday night."

He found out, and when he did he breathed her name between cries of ecstasy. And now it was his turn to gaze at the stars.

They proceeded through the entire lost week, and neither of them—at any moment—wanted to back out of the proceedings.

14

"I CAN'T COUNT THE STARS," Holly whispered dreamily. "There are too many." They were lying side by side on the white blanket. Holly was wearing Stephen's clothes. She hadn't been cold but Stephen had insisted, so she put the corduroy jacket on to make him happy. That wasn't enough for him, though. He slipped his beige slacks over her legs and hips while she was lying down. She laughed and protested that she didn't need them, but Stephen was not interested in her objections.

So, with slacks that extended past her bare feet and jacket sleeves that came almost to her fingertips, she lay beside her naked lover and gazed at countless stars. Then Holly turned on her side toward Stephen. She traced the line of his jaw with a finger that poked halfway out of a sleeve and asked, "What are you thinking about?"

"About our getting married."

"Really?"

"Yes. About that, and about the first time I saw you. I keep switching back and forth between the two. It's nice."

"Tell me what you were thinking about our getting married."

"Mmm, I was thinking that maybe we shouldn't wait for your brother and sister-in-law to get back from Mexico. Maybe we should—"

Holly nearly yelped with joy. She expressed herself further by climbing on top of him.

"Should we celebrate by breaking out the cider?" Stephen asked. "And by the way, you owe me an explanation for why you didn't bring champagne."

Holly placed her hands on the sides of his head. How she loved to gaze at him, to look at and drink in the male beauty of his features and the great human worth that shone from him. Could someone really want to harm him? It seemed impossible. She had not put it out of her mind entirely, but she didn't feel so terribly frightened now. While looking into his eyes she believed that she and Stephen were meant to be together, to live happily with the child she was carrying. And so they would.

It was time to tell him. "I didn't buy champagne because it's not good for the baby. Stephen, we're going to be parents."

He didn't say a word at first. He placed a hand on her belly, and there was a look of mingled awe and joy in his eyes. "My God, I'm so happy," he finally murmured. "I'm... I don't know how to tell you with words, Holly."

"I don't need words. Your eyes told me." She dipped her face down to his and kissed him. When he asked how long she had known, she said, "Since we were walking back to the car that first night. No, seriously, I went to the doctor's this morning. I wanted to call and tell you, but...."

She didn't finish, and when she saw a look of regret flicker in Stephen's gaze she was sorry she'd alluded to the lack of communication that had so recently existed between them. Quickly she said, "When I got home from my appointment I celebrated by dabbing some of the most expensive perfume in the world right where your hand is now, and I told the baby, 'Your father bought this for us.' I didn't tell Linda I'm pregnant. I was dying to, but couldn't. You had to be the first to know."

"Come here, Holly. Lie down on top of me. Oh, God, I love you so."

She leaned her face down to his and kissed him again, lingeringly. Then she did as he had asked. After they had rested awhile in silence, Stephen murmured, "You need to rest. Let me help you go to sleep now."

Holly knew that if she faced the miraculous display of stars there would be no possibility of falling asleep. She lay down on her stomach, feeling that even without the starry panorama, yielding to sleep would be difficult.

But Stephen helped her. He knelt astride her tenderly and began to massage her shoulders. Holly closed her eyes and basked in his touch. Her arms encircled her head, and the slight masculine aroma emanating from Stephen's jacket made her feel doubly caressed by him. He massaged her. She let her mind be at peace. He continued to massage. She slept.

"I CAN'T DECIDE what to tell Linda first," Holly mused to Stephen. They were standing in the driveway, having just stepped out of their cars.

"Mmm, the order of preference would probably be to say 'We're getting married,' first, and 'We're having a baby,' second," Stephen suggested.

Holly laughingly agreed, then said, "If she's still asleep, let's not wake her."

Holly was once again wearing the red evening dress and Stephen was in the same clothes he had worn the night before, though they were now rumpled. Holly hadn't been able to wash yesterday's makeup off her face. Stephen had a covering of stubble on his jaw and above his lip.

"I hope she is still asleep," Stephen said, "so we can sneak into the shower and put on some clean clothes. Do you suppose your brother left something behind that I can wear?"

Holly smiled, because Hank was four inches shorter than Stephen's six-foot-two, and much to her brother's dismay, had a bit of a paunch. She reminded Stephen of Hank's build, but added that she had a gift waiting for him that would solve the problem.

"I bought it for when you were supposed to spend the weekend," she confided. "It's a robe. You can put it on while I wash and dry your clothes. Anyhow, don't worry about Linda seeing you the way you are now, because she probably won't. She needs nine hours of sleep at night, and if she doesn't get to bed early she always sleeps in. On a night before we're going diving, she's actually in bed by eight o'clock."

But Linda was up, and Holly could tell that the pinched look of worry on her friend's face was not from seeing one makeup-smudged and one unshaven face in front of her.

"Linda, what's wrong? You didn't stay up all night worrying, did you?" Holly asked with concern.

"I... no, I didn't stay up. The phone rang a while ago and woke me. I've given all the birds fresh water and seed. So... who wants coffee? You two look like you could use some."

Holly thought Linda sounded like a nervous wreck, but she wasn't going to pursue it. If Linda wanted to keep something to herself, it was her right. "Who called?" she asked lightly. She would find a way to make up for having caused her friend to worry.

A look of indecision crossed Linda's face, as if she was thinking how best to answer the simple question. Without meeting Holly's eyes she said, "Oh... it was a wrong number."

Holly said she was sorry, because she knew how much Linda liked to sleep in. "Let me go make the coffee and fix breakfast," she suggested. "You sit and relax and get to know Stephen."

"Sure. I've been looking forward to that," Linda said.

Holly thought that Linda's voice sounded carefully cheerful, which meant it was as lifeless as stone. This was very strange, because Linda was usually percolating with excitement and good cheer. To brighten the mood Holly said, "Stephen doesn't usually look bedraggled, by the way. He looks the way he does because I slept in his clothes."

"Holly!" Stephen admonished. But he grinned before looking down at himself, and saying, "I could get used to a style of...should we call it 'casual inelegance'?"

Holly laughed and said they should call it "casual disaster." "I'll fix breakfast, but first I'm going to wash my face and brush my teeth. When casual inelegance extends to my teeth, it's going too far."

She left Stephen and Linda standing together in the family room. Linda was acting very unlike herself, but Holly was confident that Stephen would put her at ease. *When I come back she'll be her regular bubbly self,* Holly thought, as she closed the bathroom door.

But when she returned to the family room, Linda did not look more relaxed. Stephen looked grim. The two were seated facing each other: Stephen on the sofa; Linda on a chair. Linda was leaning forward, rubbing her hands together as if she was cold.

"What's the matter?" Holly asked, looking from one solemn face to the other.

But even as the words left her lips, Holly knew the gloom that had settled over the people she loved had something to do with the person who wanted to kill Stephen. She had a fierce yearning to protect him, and Linda, too, from the monster who was destroying their happiness and peace of mind. Because she was powerless to do so, rage rose in her breast until it was like a palpable, suffocating thing. The physical pain was real, but exhibiting it would do nothing to help, so as calmly as possible, Holly walked to the sofa and sat down beside Stephen. "He called again, didn't he?" she asked in a clear even tone.

The look in Stephen's eyes said that he was grateful; that he was proud of her. He took her hand between both of his before answering. "Linda just told me the call that woke her wasn't a wrong number. It was another threat. I've told Linda the whole story, and I called Detective Robbins. He's as concerned as I am that the man obviously knows about you and called here. He's coming over in a while."

Holly sat still digesting this information, then looked at Linda. "What did he say, Lin?"

"He thought I was you, and he said he was going to kill my boyfriend. That's all. 'I'm going to kill your boyfriend.' Then he hung up."

"Stephen? What are we going to do? I'm trying very hard...but I'm so scared and so angry." Holly felt as if she were talking without breathing, and her chest hurt so much she couldn't go on.

He drew her to him and made her rest her head on his shoulder. He stroked her hair for a moment. "I know how hard you're trying, darling, and how scared you really are. Your courage is magnificent."

"I'm scared, too," Holly heard Linda say in a small voice. "I wish you would both come back to Laguna with me. Please, would you do that?"

Holly pressed her face against Stephen's throat. "Stephen, let's go with Linda. Please."

She didn't move while waiting for his answer. There was nothing sweeter in the world, she felt, than to have your face against the warm masculine throat of the man you loved. She would not have physically displayed her love for Stephen in front of Linda under ordinary circumstances; she felt uncomfortable when other women climbed all over their men in front of her. But these weren't ordinary circumstances. And Linda was so close to her, so much a part of her life, that she certainly understood Holly's deep need to be close to Stephen now.

Stephen stroked her hair some more. Holly knew he was pondering what to do. She didn't say another word about going to Laguna. The decision was his to make. He had heard Linda's invitation, and he knew that the woman in his arms wanted him to accept it. Now it was up to him. Whatever he chose to do, Holly told herself sternly, she would accept without quarrel.

But it was hard to wait. It was maddening.

Linda broke the silence. "Stephen, won't you come, at least for a few days? And if you won't do that, surely you realize you can't stay in your house."

Stephen drew in a deep breath, and before he let it out he moved Holly back from him a little, so he could look at her face. Holly saw unrelenting determination in his eyes. She lost all her resolve. She was not going to docilely abide by Stephen's wishes.

"Holly, will you help me by doing whatever I ask you to do?"

"Yes, as long as you don't ask me to leave you." She knew what he intended without his even saying it. He wanted her to go to Laguna without him. The look in his eyes confirmed her suspicion. Oh, his damned courage! And his blasted commitment to his clients!

The phone rang just then and Holly nearly jumped

out of her skin. Linda stared at the phone and put a hand to her chest.

"Let me," Stephen said firmly. He was already reaching for the phone on the cocktail table. A steeliness had come into his features, and the muscles in his jaw were clenched in fury. He looked so volatile Holly thought the phone would be crushed by the pressure of his grip.

"Hello!" Stephen barked.

Then his features softened. He identified himself quickly in a friendly tone. Holly could tell that he was trying to sound untroubled, even cheerful. In another moment she realized Stephen was talking to her brother.

"She's right here," Stephen said. "I'll put her on." Then, "Good talking to you, too, Hank." He listened to something Hank said, then chuckled slightly and promised that he'd say hello to Daisy for him.

Holly took the phone and began the strangest conversation she'd ever had with anyone. Hank asked how the babies were and about all the good times he imagined Holly and Stephen were having together. Holly talked about parrots and the weather and ordinary things that mattered to people who weren't coming apart at the seams. She felt as if she was unraveling, and she didn't know what to do to stop the process. She wanted to blurt out to Hank that Stephen's life was in danger, and that Stephen wouldn't listen to her. She wanted to cry, "You talk some sense into him, Hank! Tell him to get on a plane and fly down there to stay with you!"

She wanted to tell her brother, also, that she was expecting Stephen's baby, and that she and Stephen were getting married. But good news seemed so inappropriate right now. She talked some more about mundane matters, assured Hank that taking care of the parrots wasn't too much work and didn't interfere with her having fun with Stephen, and said goodbye.

"We should go down there," Holly said, as she let go of the receiver and sank back against the sofa. "They're living in a very interesting village. A family therapist could learn a lot by seeing how families in another culture are structured." When Stephen didn't comment she added, "I'd treat to the tickets." She said it with a sigh, though, because it wasn't going to happen.

"Holly, you are going to Laguna with Linda."

"I am not. I won't go without you."

Stephen put his hand under her chin and lifted her face to make her look at him. He didn't sound angry, but he sounded very sure when he said, "Then you're going to make this even harder for me. You are going to cause me a lot of unnecessary worry, and—"

"I'll go," she interrupted. She kept herself from crying but burrowed against his throat again for comfort. It was small comfort.

IN AN HOUR Holly and Linda were ready to leave. They were all outside on the driveway. Stephen had put the suitcases in their cars. He had promised to look after the parrots with as much commitment as he felt toward his clients. Even more. "I don't cover my clients at night," he joked. "I'll start teaching Daisy something new to say. Maybe Daisy and Lulu could learn to harmonize 'Here Comes the Bride.'"

"Don't try to cheer me up, because you aren't going to," Holly reproached him. "Be sure to call me tonight."

"I will."

"And first thing tomorrow morning."

"I'll even throw in an extra call at noon since you're being so cooperative," he promised.

Holly was just about to get inside her car when another car pulled up and stopped in front of the house.

"That's Detective Robbins," Stephen told her. He turned and called, "Hi, Wally. You arrived just in time to meet my fiancée and our friend before they leave town."

"Don't you worry about him, miss," the detective said to Holly after Stephen had made the introductions. "We're not going to let anything happen to him."

"I want him to come away with us, but he won't listen to me," Holly confided to the burly, graying detective. She couldn't help noticing how big his gut was, thinking that he ought to take up serious swimming.

"He wouldn't listen to me before, either, but he's going to start listening now."

"How so?" Stephen asked, raising his brows in question. He folded his arms over his chest in the typical posture of a person who intends to firmly stand his ground.

"We're going to tap your phone, doctor, and I don't want to hear one word of opposition from you."

"Just be quiet and listen to him, Stephen," Holly said, although Stephen hadn't even opened his mouth to speak. She knew whose side she was on. She moved a step closer to Detective Robbins.

"You said you have a Universal Gym at your place?" the detective asked.

Stephen nodded.

"Good. I could use some exercise." The detective hooked a thumb in his belt, calling attention to his girth. "I'm moving in tonight, after supper."

"Now, wait just a minute," Stephen said forcefully, and he shook his head as emphatically as Holly had ever seen a head being shaken. "You know my feelings about your—"

"I know, I know," the detective interrupted. "You don't want me to take your place as the sitting duck. All right, I won't. You'll be there, too. We'll both be sitting ducks. But I think our bozo is getting ready to make a move, and I'm danged well sure I'm going to be around when he does."

"That's very good thinking, Detective Robbins," Holly said. She liked this man more every minute.

"Thank you, Miss Hutton. I think the case is going to be resolved soon, and you and the doctor here won't have this guy to worry about anymore."

Holly wanted to kiss him. Instead she shook his hand warmly and told him it had been very good meeting him. "I can't thank you enough for the reassurance you've given me," she said sincerely. "I'm much less frightened now."

"Well, that's good to hear. Tell you what. You thank me by inviting me to your wedding."

"Yours will be the first invitation in the mail," Holly said softly.

Stephen put an arm around her and squeezed her shoulder. Now she was willing to get in the car and leave. She still didn't want to, but she didn't feel as miserable about departing as she had a few minutes ago. There were more goodbyes. There were kisses. There were waves. She was on the road.

15

THE DRIVE FROM PALM SPRINGS to Laguna would take approximately two and one-half hours, depending on traffic. For about twenty minutes everything made sense to Holly. She was on her way to Laguna where she would be safe, and because she would be safe much of the burden of worry would be lifted from Stephen's shoulders. Stephen would stay in his own home at night in the protective company of a competent detective. By day he would live normally, adding to his routine the care of Hank and Nettie's parrots. He would call Holly two or three times a day so she would know he was still alive. If the man who wanted to kill him made his move—as Detective Robbins had put it—and events went according to plan, the man would soon be apprehended and locked up. Stephen would not be hurt.

If events went according to plan. If. Holly started thinking about the "ifs," which in this case were plentiful enough to think about for the rest of the drive to Laguna.

First, what if the man didn't make a move? What if he never did? Perhaps he intended to continue threatening Stephen forever. That wasn't so far-fetched. He might know how much stress he was causing with the threats; he might intend to keep on causing it.

What then? Did she stay in Laguna forever? Did Stephen live alone indefinitely so nobody he loved would ever be in danger?

There was another, more-disturbing "if" to think about. What if the man was ready to strike, as Detective Robbins thought he was? If he did, whatever the outcome, she wouldn't be there. She would be snug and safe in Laguna. She would not be beside Stephen at the moment his life was imperiled.

She thought about these things. She drove. She wondered. The main thing she questioned was where love fit into the picture.

She tried to imagine what would have happened if their roles had been reversed. Just suppose someone had decided to kill her. Would Stephen have let himself be removed to a safe distance? Would he go off somewhere and wait for phone calls, so he could be reassured that Holly had not been harmed?

Hardly. He would not. And neither would she. She had been driving behind Linda's Volkswagen but she accelerated to change lanes and pulled up alongside her. She motioned to Linda to pull off the road. Linda indicated with a nod that she understood.

"I'm going back, Lin," she said when they were standing by the road beside their cars.

"Holly, don't. It's a mistake. We're practically at Laguna. You're going to upset him if you go back."

"Then he'll have to be upset. The worst that can happen is my not being with him when I should be."

Linda crossed her arms over her chest and looked down. She kicked a piece of gravel. "I'm afraid something will happen to you."

"I'm not. It's Stephen I'm worried about. I love him so much, Linda. I love him.... You know how sometimes, when you're down in the ocean, you think how vast and deep the sea is? That's how wide, how all-encompassing my love for Stephen is. Lin, I love him the way you love Kevin. He's the meaning in my life, and I don't want to be apart from him. Especially now."

Linda was crying, and she was not a person to cry easily. Holly seldom saw this happen. It brought a lump to her own throat. All she could do was put her arms around her friend and hug her fiercely.

"I agree with everything you said." Linda sniffed. "I'd feel the same way if Kevin's life was in danger. So go on back. Do your thing. But tell that gorgeous hunk of yours that it wasn't my fault. Tell him I tried to stop you. Say that I got you in a hammerlock and then tried to sit on you. Will you do that?"

Holly promised she would. She gave Linda's bangs a gentle tug, knowing the tug Linda felt was the one on her heart. "Take care," she said, and turned to get back into her car.

"Drive carefully!" Linda ordered sternly.

"You too. I'll call you."

When she pulled onto the pavement this time, she was one hundred percent certain she was going in the right direction.

She got a flat tire. She pulled off, or rather limped off, the road. For a long moment she just sat and felt sorry for herself. She folded her arms on the steering wheel and rested her face on them as if hiding from the nasty pranks of fate. But she knew that if she was going to get back to Palm Springs soon she would have to act. Changing a tire was something she'd never done. It wasn't that she had shied away from the task; it just hadn't come up. She had been lucky until now. The only trouble ever to have befallen her in a car was the time a bag of groceries fell off the seat and some eggs broke.

Just consider this one more carton of broken eggs, she ordered herself. Getting out of the car, she went to the trunk for the jack and spare. She worked slowly and carefully, and by some miracle even intelligently. Her hands, pants and shirt were dirty, but eventually the job was done. Before hoisting the damaged tire into the trunk of the car she gave it a swift kick, just so it would know how much it had inconvenienced her.

Then she was on the road again.

At last, after seemingly endless driving, she was in the home stretch. She thought of what she would say to placate Stephen. She doubted that pleading an overwhelming commitment to her students would be an acceptable excuse. It was one thing for him to be dedicated to his clients; he definitely wouldn't believe the equivalent fidelity was necessary of her.

She sighed. She had no good reason to present to him. She had come back because she loved him. That was not an excuse; it was fact.

She was surprised to see Stephen's car parked in her driveway. Thinking he would be at home working off some of his frustration in his gym, she hadn't expected to have to confront him until this evening. She needed a bit of time to herself to gird herself against Stephen's certain anger.

Well, he won't make me turn and go back. He wouldn't be that cruel, she reasoned to herself. She had been driving the better part of three hours. Stephen might be disgusted with her for returning to Palm Springs, but he would have to accede that she had driven enough for one day.

She got her suitcase and overnight bag out of the car. Neither was overly heavy, so she carried them both up the walk to the front door. It was unlocked, so she went inside and set the luggage down in the entry hall. The house was still. Where was Stephen? Surely he would have heard her car or heard the door open. Angry or not, why hadn't he come to greet her?

She considered that he might be swimming. She would go to the family room to look out the window and see if he was in the pool.

She stopped suddenly when she got to the family room. She had lost all interest in checking outside. Her eyes swept around the room, taking in the cages of various sizes. All the birds were locked up. All were staring at her. All were still and silent.

She whirled and looked at Daisy. The macaw always proclaimed "I'm in love! Love is wonderful!" when Holly came home. Always, unless there was a stranger in the house.

Holly's legs felt weak, and nausea washed over her. She felt that she needed to sit down, but there was no time to sit. Good God, was there even time to think?

Yes. She must think. She must think because whatever she did she had to do quickly and correctly. *I'll call the police.* But was there even time for the police to get there? Stephen was in the house with the assassin. She knew that there was no time.

Holly looked toward the master bedroom. Intuitively she knew that she would find them there. Slowly she started to walk. *Give me strength,* she prayed in silence. *Give me courage.*

She had never thought of herself as courageous. During the ordeal at Big Bear she had become certain of her lack of courage. She had not screamed or struck at Linda's attacker. She had not tried to wrest the gun away from him. She had been a docile, helpless victim, a passive witness to the suffering of a person she loved.

Not again. Not this time. This time I'll count for something.

She was at the closed bedroom door. From within the room came only earsplitting silence. From her chest came the sound of kettledrums. For the briefest second, before she closed a hand over the doorknob, she placed that hand on her abdomen. *We will not be hurt,* she vowed from her soul. The we meant three people. She put her hand on the knob and turned it.

HE WAS ORDINARY LOOKING. "We kept quiet in here so you'd go away," he said gruffly. "You should have gone, lady."

The man was standing, holding a gun. Stephen was seated in a chair by the window. His hands were tied behind the chair and his running shoes were laced together.

"You shouldn't have seen me," the man said.

Then Stephen spoke. In a clear, calm tone he said, "It doesn't matter. She'll forget. When your emotions are overwhelmed you don't remember a person's features."

"Maybe not," the man said. "Maybe it doesn't matter, anyhow. I'll probably do what I came here to do and then turn myself in. It doesn't matter what happens to me now that I've lost Susan."

"Then order her to leave," Stephen said.

Holly had never heard such utter calm in a voice. She wrested her gaze, which was one of almost hypnotic fear, from the man's face and looked at Stephen. He was on the verge of losing his life, and his entire concern was for her safety. While she stared at him he repeated to the man, "Give the order for her to go. She'll obey you."

"I won't. I won't leave you," Holly whispered.

"Tell her it'll be worse for me if she doesn't go," Stephen said.

This time Holly could detect the urgency of unbearable tension in Stephen's voice. She realized that he was being careful not to address her directly. He only addressed the man, to make him feel that he was the one in control even while Stephen manipulated him.

"Seems like you really care about her," the man

said. "You seduce all those wives that come to you, but this one's special, huh? Maybe I should pay you back by doing to her what you did to Susan. I'll be her lover." He took a step toward Holly, and surveyed her crudely.

"No! She isn't special, not in that sense! She came to me as a client because she has severe heart disease. I gave her counseling to help her cope with her illness, and we've become friends. That's all. The stress she's undergoing now could be fatal for her, so order her to leave. Now! Order her to go!"

The frustration had finally broken through in Stephen's voice. Then, in his anguish he spoke directly to Holly. "Leave!" he commanded angrily. "Leave this instant! Do as I say, dammit!"

The man didn't say anything. He waited. Holly felt that he didn't care if she left or not. She didn't move or utter a sound. Her eyes were riveted on Stephen's, but she was listening to the voice of another man. She could hear the words of her karate instructor as clearly as if he was in the room. *You are probably never going to use what I will teach you here, Holly, but hear me well. If you do have to use it you cannot do half a job. You cannot worry that you'll inflict crippling pain. You will do just that, because your opponent won't give you a second chance if you don't. So you will do all the damage that you can—swiftly, easily, correctly. Then you can say you're sorry and put a pillow under his head.*

The man said, "She don't obey you so good, just like Susan won't listen to me. I don't think she has a heart problem, either. Her heart might break when I use this gun on you, but right now she looks like a real healthy lady."

He walked two more steps toward the doorway where Holly stood. He'd been aiming the gun at Stephen, but now he pointed it toward the ceiling. When he took the two steps toward her he blocked her view of Stephen. She could not see her lover. She only knew that the gun was not aimed at him. He was, for this moment in time, out of danger. It was time for her to act. But the man wasn't close enough to her yet. She had to draw him nearer. She could entice him by being seductive, but he might see through that. He probably would. So there was only one tactic left to her.

"Don't touch her!" Stephen said passionately. "Please! You're not that kind of person! You're not a rapist! You're upset now, but you can get your life back on track! Basically you're a decent person! Don't touch her!"

The man ignored Stephen's pleas and kept looking at Holly.

"Please don't come near me," Holly begged, looking with wide and terrified eyes at the man. She made her lips tremble as she said, "Don't touch me. Please don't. Stephen is the only man who has ever touched me. I couldn't bear it if another man...oh, don't. Don't, please!" She ended her fervent appeal in a whimpering tone.

The man smiled at this display of raw fear. He kept the gun pointed upward.

You will do all the damage that you can—swiftly, easily, correctly.

The man took the bait. He came toward her.

HOLLY KNELT DOWN behind Stephen to untie his hands. It was not easy to do, because her own hands were shaking so much. She had put the gun down on the nightstand beside the chair, and when Stephen's hands were freed she picked it up gingerly and handed it to him. "Hold it on him," she begged with a shudder. "I'll call the police."

"Honey, I don't think I need to hold this thing. He's unconscious. You'd better tell the police to send paramedics, too." There was incredulity in Stephen's tone when he spoke, and he was looking at Holly with something akin to awe.

Holly asked Stephen to hold the gun on the man anyway, saying, "His being here scares me even if he is unconscious." She used the phone on the nightstand to call the police. Then she knelt to untie Stephen's shoelaces. Her hands still shook. She thought she'd better tie each one. Stephen couldn't hold a gun and do up his shoes at the same time, and she didn't want him to stand up and trip on a lace. So she tried repeatedly to tie his shoelaces.

She couldn't. The frustration of not being able to, plus all that had happened, hit her suddenly and hard. She put her head on Stephen's lap and clung to his legs. She heard the gun being placed on the nightstand, and she wanted to tell Stephen not to put it down—that he must continue to hold it on the man. But she couldn't talk. She couldn't talk and she couldn't cry. First he caressed her head and the back of her neck, and then he was pulling her up off the floor.

"Get up here where you belong," he said. She did,

but when she was on his lap she whispered, "Hold the gun on him, Stephen. Please."

He drew her against him tightly, and when her face was pressed against the comfort of his throat he said, "Holly, forget the gun. He can't move. I'm so shocked by what you did *I* can hardly move. Why didn't you tell me you knew karate?"

"I don't know. It just never fit into the conversation. Stephen, even if he can't move, it scares me to be in the same room with him."

"Okay, we'll go to another room to wait for the police. But I promise you that if he comes around, the last thing he'll want is to be in the same room with you."

Holly got off his lap, instructing, "Tie your shoes before you get up. You'll trip."

He shook his head and asked in wonder, "What did I do before I had you to take care of me?" He tied his shoes. Then, holding hands, they walked from the room. Holly didn't want to see the man lying on the floor. Stephen looked. "He's still breathing, but when he wakes up he's going to wish he wasn't," he said. "I still can't believe what I saw. Honey, it was just incredible. Will you teach me karate?"

"No! I never want to do it again!" They were in the hallway. Stephen put an arm around her shoulders and she leaned against him.

"They're here," Stephen said at the sounds of car doors opening and people rushing to the door.

When Detective Robbins came out of the bedroom he looked at Holly with undisguised amazement. "You did that?" he asked.

She nodded.

"Who was your teacher? Where is he?"

She told him.

"We're going to have to get hold of that fellow—have him give the whole force lessons." The detective watched as paramedics carried the man out on a stretcher.

Holly turned her head toward Stephen, so she wouldn't have to look.

"I'm going to give you some time alone together. But you'll have to come down to the station. Don't be surprised if people stand up and cheer when you come in, Miss Hutton. You're a real heroine."

"We appreciate the time, Wally. We'll be there in an hour or so," Stephen said.

"Okay. So long." The detective started to leave but turned back and looked at Holly. "Gosh darn, I wish I'd been here. I'd have given anything to see that," he said wistfully. Then he brightened and said, "But seeing you two when you say your 'I dos' will be just as good, maybe better." He left.

"Stephen, I don't want to be alone here tonight."

"There's no chance that you're going to be. You're coming home with me. And this time you're going to remember to cover the cages first."

They were spending the time Detective Robbins had granted them wisely. Stephen was lying on his back on the family-room sofa. Holly was lying on top of him. After a few moments of snuggling in silence Holly said, "I was thinking about our getting married."

"Mmm, what?"

"Let's do it right away. We don't need a big wedding."

"You don't want the excitement of planning and shopping and talking to caterers and choosing your attendants? All the fuss and bother and hoopla?"

"Darling, I don't want any excitement at all, except the excitement of our lovemaking."

Stephen sighed deeply, and when he did Holly rose like a raft on a gentle wave. "That's the kind of excitement I like best, too," he murmured. "But we promised Wally he'd be going to a wedding."

"He will be. We'll have a beautiful, small, intimate affair. Your folks and mine, Linda and Kevin, your best friend...Stephen, I don't even know who that is. Who's your best friend?"

"You."

Holly smiled, and kissed his chest. "You're mine, too," she said. "So we'll have just those people and Detective Robbins. Okay?"

Stephen lay still. He felt the sweet weight of Holly on top of him. He could feel the beat of her heart and the breaths she took in and let out. Because of the perfect way her body fit over his, he could feel every part of her—even where their child was being nurtured. He was as relaxed as he was ever going to be in his lifetime; he felt as rewarded by life as it was humanly possible to be. But he also felt greedy. He wanted something else.

Reaching over Holly he grabbed the phone and called the detective. He said that if it didn't make any difference he would rather come down to Wally's office in the morning, he was tired and wanted to relax. The detective said that would be fine. Stephen asked, "Are you off duty next Sunday? How would you like to come to a wedding?" He listened to a few things the detective had to tell him, and then got off the phone.

"He said to tell you the guy's okay. He woke up, and he's begging to be locked up in a nice safe room somewhere. They're going to accommodate him."

Holly breathed a sigh of relief.

"Get undressed," Stephen said. He grinned at her.

Holly looked surprised. "You told him you were tired and wanted to relax."

"Just do as I say, my love. When a woman has saved a man's life the man has a right to give her orders."

"Are you sure?" Holly tried to look skeptical, but in the meantime she began to get out of her clothes.

Stephen did likewise. Holly watched him as he undressed, and he watched her. She put her clothes in a neat pile on the cocktail table, with her shirt folded on top. Stephen did the same, with his shirt on the bottom. One alligator climbing playfully on top of another.

"What now?" Holly asked, as he took her hand.

He looked into the sea-blue eyes that mesmerized his soul. They were truly the eyes of a mermaid. "Now, my beautiful mermaid, we swim."

They went outside, but Stephen remembered that they would need towels later. He watched Holly execute an exquisite dive, then went back inside to get them. As he walked through the family room,

Daisy, with all the gusto she could muster, sang out: "I'm in love! Love is wonderful! I'm in love! Love is wonnnderfullllll!"

"Better believe it, Daisy."

What romance fans say about Harlequin...

"...scintillating, heartwarming... a very important, integral part of mass-market literature."

—J.G.,* San Antonio, Texas

"...it is a pleasure to escape behind a Harlequin and go on a trip to a faraway country."

—B.J.M., Flint, Michigan

"Their wonderfully depicted settings make each and every one a joy to read."

—H.B., Jonesboro, Arkansas

*Names available on request.